**PURE
SLUSH
BOOKS**

Pure Slush Vol. 10

First published January 2016

Stories copyright © Pure Slush and individual authors
Edited by Matt Potter

Pure Slush Books
4 Warburton Street
Magill SA 5072
Australia

Email: edpureslush@live.com.au
Website: http://pureslush.webs.com
Visit the Pure Slush Store: http://pureslush.webs.com/store.htm

Cover and title page illustrations copyright © Allen Forrest

ISBN: 978-1-925101-71-3

Also available as an eBook:
ISBN: 978-1-925101-72-0

A note on differences in punctuation and spelling

Pure Slush proudly features (both online and in print) writers from all over the English-speaking world. Some speak and write English as their first language, while for others, it's their second or third or even fourth language. Naturally, across all versions of English, there are differences in punctuation and spelling, and even in meaning. These differences are reflected in the work *Pure Slush* publishes, and it accounts for any differences in punctuation, spelling and meaning found within these pages.

There is nothing much
to say beyond

Five years!

and to dedicate
this book
to all those
who have contributed
to Pure Slush
online and in print
since 6th December 2010

Almost Transparent
by Len Kuntz

I'm ovulating and that's a good thing, my husband says.

He wants to have a baby.

The only problem is that every night my husband and I make love I see the other five.

Sometimes they are streaks and shadows. Other times they are fully-formed and real: the men who once had me in college, by force.

My husband says our sex life is getting stale. He proposes going to a sex store together. He says, "Don't look so worried. It'll be fun!" That last lift in his voice reeks of desperation and insecurity and excitement all at once.

"I don't think so," I say.

"Come on. You said we should be transparent about our feelings, our wants and desires. So I do what you recommend and you just shut me down?"

I go with him to a place called Lovers, a squat building wearing a cheerful purple logo with the "v" in the shape of a heart.

Inside there are racks of school girl outfits and crocheted outfits with a hole near the crotch. There are soft-core and hard-core DVDs for sale, which is surprising considering we've had the internet all this time.

There are every size and shape and length of dildos and vibrators, some that glow, some that don't.

There are handcuffs banded with feathers, and handcuffs strictly made of steel.

There are ball-gags.

Fanny paddles.

And hot wax kits.

DIY genitalia piercing kits.

And latex spacemen-looking suits.

The thing that stops me, though, is the glow-in-the-dark condoms. On one hook is a full set that is supposed to make the color purple glow.

Somehow, even back then, the fraternity boys had gotten hold of rubbers that glowed purple once the condoms met with the heat that skin gives off.

These boys were rough and awful, but they were also cautious.

They took turns, and reset, taking turns again.

They were young but brutal.

Afterward, the next day, no one believed me.

"These boys are good boys," I was told.

"These boys have good parents. They're ambitious, going to be future lawyers and senators," I was told.

"Let's get a row of them," I tell my husband now at the sex toy store named Lovers.

He looks like a sad old dog, suddenly jowly. "Just that? *That's* all you want?"

"Yep," I say.

He scratches the back of his head, his eyes turned to bees working over the tiled floor.

"Okay," he says. "For now, but maybe later we won't need them?"

I don't answer, just pluck the packets free.

Back at home, we barely make it to the bedroom and our clothes are off in a blink and I won't let my husband turn on the lights like he always wants to do when we have sex.

"Put it on," I say, meaning the condom which turns purple as he applies it.

"As a matter of fact," I say, "use two."

Five Damsels for Good Luck
by Mira Desai

Sarita had known her mother-in-law would go overboard at the naming ceremony for her newborn. An infant welcomed into the Ajmera fold after years of despair. That too a son, an heir to the family's fortunes. The mansion dazzled with red and gold lights, strands of jasmine and marigold decked the halls, lamps were lit to all the Gods and the scent of rich ghee diffused from the kitchen. Guests from all over India and a few continents would begin to arrive shortly. New clothes had been bought for everyone, matching silks for her sisters-in-law, new uniforms for the servants and drivers. Jewellery had been brought out from padlocked trunks.

"Finally an heir to the Ajmera fortunes, the inheritor of all our abundance...," her mother-in-law had said, with tears in her eyes. At such times Sarita could forget the taunts she had been subject to for much too long.

"We must remember to invite five *goranis*, five young girls not more than seven years old... at that age, they're pure, reincarnation of the Mother Goddess... we must give them the same respect. Bring luck to the child, our successor..."

"Five silver coins in five boxes lined with plush red velvet for the Mother Goddess..." Sarita said, taking notes and looking away.

For this was a direct descendant, all right. Only that science had done its bit to assist, after all the visits to the astrologers and holy men proved to be in vain.

As had her father-in-law. Not that anyone would ever
know.

Pre-K
by Mark Danowsky

My earliest memory is more of
an image, a scene really
in which I am in a field at the JCC
and spot a pale green praying mantis
almost as tall as the child
one moment playing in the wood chips
under the monkey bars of
the candy red rubberized jungle gym
then suddenly approaching, waving
a stick

Five Finger Exercise Redux
by Susan Tepper

When I carry the dirty plate back to the cut out window of the coffee shop kitchen, behind which Joey Largesse is frying, he flashes a big toothy grin. "I can get you into movies."

From off the dirty plate I toss a half-eaten dinner roll at his head. He ducks. "You could start as a fluffer. You're gorgeous. But you have no resumé. You need to work your way up in the biz."

Chucking the plate and silverware into the wash bin I say, "Isn't a fluffer a type of fish?"

"That's a puffer." Joey laughs like crazy waving his hand like *are you dumb or what*. Unfortunately, a hand with four fingers. Middle finger left hand chopped off while he diced an onion during a lunchtime rush.

"Honey-cakes. Naïve princess. A *fluffer* keeps the talent ready between takes." Joey deliberately looking down at what I know is his sizeable bulge.

Who could miss that thing? Huge even squashed into jeans behind a greasy apron. "Wait. Are you suggesting I give blow jobs to porn stars? Is that what you're saying?"

"It beats slinging hash and you *are* gorgeous. You could work your way up in a few weeks, less even. This how you want to spend your best years?" Despite missing a finger, he tosses a mini-pizza with finesse.

I hiss through the kitchen cut out. "I have my college tuition to pay off, why do you think I hang around this dump?"

He grins again. A grinning idiot, my mom would say and plenty more if she heard his proposition.

Peppering some kind of meat, one side then the other, Joey shrugs. "Have it your way."

"How can you, um, well, perform without five fingers?" It is a fair question.

Normally we wouldn't be having this conversation. The owner John Tim would be watching over everything hawk-like. Today is his appendectomy.

"Lighting. Camera angles. They know they've got a star here. What's a missing finger compared with a schlong like mine?" He rings the food bell even though I'm standing two feet away. "Table seven. Think about it, Lila. You even have the perfect name. They could dub your scene *Lila in Love*."

I grab the plates of burgers and fries. "You disgust me."

"I disgust me." Joey smirks. "You can't beat the money. Out of debt in a year, Lila my love."

"Don't ever call me that."

I deliver the food to table seven. A moment later the man is gesturing madly with his arm. Returning to their table, he's poking at his burger. "I ordered medium-rare. This is so well done it could be dead."

For some reason I focus on his hand. Five fingers. The other hand, too. The stringy wife with the grey streak up her part is hovering, bitching. Is this what happens from too many coffee shop meals?

My face suddenly tight like a mask. "It's supposed to be dead. Maybe you prefer eating live cow?"

Sashiko
by Alex Reece Abbott

It's my act of devotion, making your patched jacket.

I guard your back with my small, even stitches, binding the layers so that needlecraft's secret code follows the grain of fabric. I can read the squares on the waistcoat of a rice-man.

Go to work with a dragon, a rabbit hero on your back, safe in your hard-wearing work-wear. I have a hundred stitches up my sleeve – extra protection for you. Across your heart, that dense hypnotic pattern wards off evil spirits as easily as the cold and the rain. I'll repel all the serpents and spiders with persimmon brown, use indigo blue for strength. I'll pack your bodice with memories, old times, ancient messages; that way I'll always be with you.

You can show off my skills to your friends, both of us knowing that we'll never rise above cotton, never slip on some forbidden silk.

Again and again, I'll replace your neck, your collar, your sleeves. Stitch and patch and grind down cloth, worn and weather-beaten as your body. I'll unpick your jacket to wash it, then reconstruct it, piece by piece. Precious, precious, best graded rags. I'll recycle the past until there is no more, then your ragged coat will become my duster.

I'm a farm-girl, only judged wife-worthy after I delivered five samples of my handiwork. Proven fit for the family work-force, home made.

Home maid.

*

Outside, a gale is howling tonight.

I'm stitching you up, keeping you warm with my parallel lines. So warm. How easily you'll move in your jacket, heavy yet soft. My stitches hold strong power, even Enola Gay's flames couldn't touch you, not now you're protected by me.

I wear my disposition on my sleeve and pass down my stitching skills. We'll be self-sufficient until West-is-Best tears through us, suddenly ashamed to be seen in home-made patchwork.

Go husband, work the ocean in all weathers.

Go, work by day and by night. Be absent – I've got my eye on you, husband. I'm holding you with my threads, keeping you safe in stormy seas.

Your story recorded in tiny threads, until your shape becomes a ghost's proof rubbed on your coat.

After an exhibition curated by Michele Walker, from the collection from Fukuoka City Museum.

Cinco de Mayo
by Todd McKie

I was in no mood for a party, but Leah said, C'mon, it'll be fun. We won't know anybody, I said. That's what parties are for, she said, to meet new people.

The Nordlingers were throwing the party. Rachel Nordlinger works with Leah and Grant's a successful veterinarian. Are they inviting his patients? I said. Very funny, said Leah.

It's festive attire, said Leah, so please don't dress like you're going to the office. I chose a yellow shirt I'd never worn before, one I'd bought because Leah claimed every piece of clothing I owned made me look like an accountant. So what? I'd said at the time, I *am* an accountant.

They're having a mariachi band, said Leah. Great, I said, I love that music. Don't be sarcastic, said Leah.

When we arrived the party was in full swing. Hola, said Rachel. Bienvenidos, amigos, said Grant. Rachel wore a long, embroidered dress and tons of turquoise jewelry. Her husband wore tan slacks with a huge silver belt buckle, a western shirt, cowboy boots, and a string tie.

Grant said, Grab a cerveza, amigo. We've got muchos margaritas too. Hope you kids wore your dancing shoes, this could get loco.

Inside, strings of tiny Mexican flags hung everywhere. I gulped a couple of beers, then switched to margaritas.

Except for the mariachis—six guys in fancy black suits and sombreros—there weren't any actual Mexicans at the party. The mariachis were on the terrace, sawing on fiddles, slashing at guitars, blowing horns and hollering, Ai, ai, ai, ai!

Leah said, Let's dance! but I couldn't get the hang of it. Loosen up, for God's sake, she said. Feel that Latin rhythm.

I don't recall tripping over an electric cord and smashing my head into one of the amps. When I came to, worried faces wobbled above me. Leah's swam into focus. She said, You're bleeding! and, Somebody get a doctor! I guess there wasn't a real doctor at the party because soon Grant helped me to my feet, saying, It's only a superficial flesh wound, amigo. He pressed a decorative paper napkin against my forehead. Somebody led me to a chair. The band plugged in again. My head was throbbing and when the trumpets started blasting it felt like someone had hammered a spike into it.

Grant wrapped gauze around my head. A woman said, Take off your shirt, we'll pour club soda on it. I didn't care about my shirt, and I sure as hell wasn't taking it off. I wanted to go home.

Our host and hostess stood in the driveway as we walked to the car, Leah guiding me by the hand because the bandage had slipped down over my eyes. Grant hollered, Happy Cinco de Mayo! and, See you next year!

Fat fucking chance, amigo, I muttered. We got in the car, an unhappy woman and a wounded man. Leah drove us home.

Karma Sutra – Rotisserie Style
by R. Gerry Fabian

You skewer my heart
and slow cook it
over a slow revolving
fire circle of passion.

No flame broil,
bake at 450,
boiling pot
or
pan sear burn
for you.

You want an even seared
outer crust
with juice dripping
time tested roasted heart.

When the appropriate
time occurs,
you devour me
like a ravaged heathen.

Angling
by Jolene McIlwain

She woke one morning—after a dream about her fisherman friend, Van, who'd died too young—with the sensation of a hook snagged on the inside of her cheek, close to her lip. Like a piece of fishing line attached from her drooped mouth to him, wherever he lingered now.

Her son didn't catch it at first, and when she slurred, "Does my mouth look right," he answered, "Yeah, you look fine, Mom." But he also wrinkled his brows and turned his eyes to his father, saying, in a tone she rarely heard now that he was growing into a man, "Daaaad."

Her husband worried she'd stroked. Her father had one, and her grandfather, grandmother, and three uncles. He called 911, promised he'd be right behind her, and before they lifted her into the ambulance, he kissed her good side.

The doctor assured, "It's not a stroke. It's temporary."

"What about my eye?" She said. "It won't stop crying."

He marked, with a lopsided star, 'excessive tearing' on the list of symptoms he handed her. "Two weeks. You'll be back to normal."

But she knew what happened. Van had caught her again, just when she thought she'd been healed of him, and she peered out the window as her husband drove them back home along Route 5 and that winding flooded creek bed where she'd once talked too much and spooked the rainbow and brook trout, sending them into deeper runs.

Had Van used a dressed treble hook, meant to lure her with its flashy feathers, or a siwash, meant to leave her less damaged by his memory, or a jig hook to ensure the set?

She could see his smile, his eyes, almost touch his fingers again as he crimped five split shot to the line to weight it down.

After the two weeks her doctor promised, her face righted and Van's face faded again, rippled back to blurs, caught deep in a back-cast, tangled in a tree she couldn't find.

Waiting for My Wife Who's Gone to do a Quick Errand
by Tim Suermondt

Five seconds. It didn't take long to miss her,
no one does the instants better than me.

It's a cold day and a man down the street
is actually making a bonfire, looking responsible

in the way he starts the flame.
I open the refrigerator, searching for a snack

that is hiding itself well, but I persevere
and find it, untouched, to my delight.

Time quickens with every bite I take, the sound
of a key turning in the door becomes the universe,

my wife arriving fresh as a new planet,
announcing she's back like she never meant to leave.

Impossible Sonata
by Heather McQuillan

Dr. Daumen tapped his fingers on the glass as the delivery nurse counted fingers and toes. Each exceeded the customary five.

"Perfecto," the mother tremoloed, her vocal chords swollen by labour.

"Just as ordered! Bravo, Daumen!" said the father, applauding.

Daumen bowed, backed through the door and left them to their engineered joy to return to the cool calm of chemicals and nucleotide sequences. A reporter called for comment but the geneticist pulled his coat collar up and bundled on. *What would Elsa say?* He turned back but the opportunity was gone. Shouts arose from beneath the balcony as the composer held his bawling daughter aloft, her fame-destined fingers hidden within stubborn fists. The paparazzi's frustrations were muttered in accented expletives.

A wit called out, "She has her mother's lungs!"

The cameras turned clicking, piranhas eager for flesh.

Daumen understood the risk of leaving sperm and egg to collide in thoughtless conception. His first born... but there'd been no such artless fate for Elsa. Her entrepreneurial future was cultivated and refined from her very beginnings. The slogan she created, 'Perfect the Future', enticed the glitterati that graced his clinic. Healthy organs, strong straight bodies, leadership qualities, these were every parent's right. Those who demanded he sculpt tails and horns, gills, fluorescent skin, those Daumen despised, but Elsa advised him to accept their patronage. He deferred to her genetic superiority in such matters.

The Sorensons were well known among those whose cliques Elsa orbited. He'd welcomed them in.

"So, you wish me to ensure your child has the musical gene," he'd joked.

The composer feigned insult. "We can manage that ourselves."

"Music will be part of our daughter's soul," trilled the mother.

"We want six fingers on each hand!"

Their duet complete, they waited for the inevitable question. He did not ask it. He knew of the impossible sonata. Daumen drummed eight fingertips on the desk; his mind was filled with twisting strands and tiny nodules.

"There is a complication. Your daughter will also have twelve toes. I haven't yet isolated one set of digits from the other. Surgery could always be considered."

The mother waved her hand. "Bah! She will wear shoes, won't she?"

Daumen manipulated enzymes and made the splice. He threw in the negotiated extras; healthy organs, long legs and slim body. He also added his silent trademark, splicing in an

28

extra gene, a slice of intelligence from his own private store. He'd done it before, prompted by something Elsa had once whispered as he bent over his microscope.

"You are a fairy godmother bestowing gifts upon every child who comes under your gaze."

Daumen steepled his fingers beneath his second chin as he watched the composer prying out the six fingers of his daughter for the paparazzi's zooming lenses.

"What's her name?" called a reporter.

"Ebony-Ivory."

Dr. Daumen shuddered. "She will know it too." The thought choked him. "She will know she has been brought into this world by fools."

A Spring Tour of Vermont
by William Doreski

Near Quechee the smut of construction
has soiled the landscape so badly
it's lifetimes past recovery.

A faux diner ringed by a toy train
smirks on the rim of a strip mall
while a Wild West Emporium

glares with goods for the horsey set.
Its plastic knotty pine façade
frightens us all the way to Woodstock,

where crouched outside a bakery,
splitting a lemon cheese Danish,
we agree that affluent blondes

have disheartened all America,
the tread of their money so heavy
it has crushed our geography

and left us broken and writhing
like a pair of run-over squirrels.
Refueled with expensive coffee

we take a two-lane state road south
and note mobile homes still aching
in pine-shaded hollows, tin roofs

rusting on narrow frame houses
shouldered against arrogant slopes.
Damp but insistent afternoon light

still expresses shadows across
mountains sheltering deer and bear.
When we reach the river at Route Five

we're debating the merits
of writing the past so legibly
even the average politician

could read it. But the past hurts,
and as it has festered and drained
has left beneath your talk a silence

full of dark matter science can't see.
I can't place myself in that vacuum
so we drive to the authentic

and greasy diner in Windsor
where we stifle our hearts with burgers
and onion rings. Old-fashioned chrome

winks at us. The waitress totals
our check. We've resolved nothing,
neither the violated landscape

nor the warping of your childhood,
but leaving Windsor we drive across
the world's longest covered bridge

and we're grateful for these moments
of sheltering whitewashed trusses,
the river-smell richer than speech.

The Boner
by Nancy Stohlman

It was 5 o'clock rush hour and I was driving my son's best friend home from soccer practice, something I did every Wednesday and every other Friday. The car still smelled like French fries and my mind was elsewhere, wondering if I should stop for gas now or later, and whether I had enough hamburger at home for chili. Supertramp came on the radio, and I reached for the volume knob, and that's when I saw it, peeking from the bottom of his yellow running shorts.

I looked away quickly. Shit! What do I say? *Um, honey, I think your boner is showing.* No, no, don't use the word boner. How about erection? *Your erection is showing*—oh god no, I was going to embarrass him, possibly scar him. Maybe I shouldn't say anything? No, I can't let him ride the whole way home like that. I could just say *I think you might need to adjust your shorts?*

The next right turn forced eye contact with it, then him. He was staring at me without flinching, his blue eyes gazing at me as if he'd never seen me before, and I lost all my words.

Baby Needs Shoes
by Walter Giersbach

"C'mon," Tony Huang shouted, "baby need shoes." The dice bounced off the wall and he groaned. *"Bu hau!"* His last dollar was gone until he could see if Penny had any money.

"You all the time shoot craps, Tony!" Penny shouted that night in their Chinatown walkup. "I work hard and you piss away our money. Look at Didi," she pointed at the toddler playing with a pile of mah-jongg tiles. "He need clothes and baby formula and I still have to pay rent money."

Tony muttered, "I just wanted to see my friends."

"I got no money for babysitting. You have to take care of Didi. No foolin'. Tomorrow I go to work and you mind the baby."

Tony wanted to do right by Penny, but New York cost so much and he couldn't work as a baker. They wanted him to pay off the owner and prove himself before he could get a salary.

As soon as Penny left for the nail salon, he put Didi in the stroller and walked down East Broadway.

"Hey, Big Guy," Albert shouted. Albert spoke mostly Cantonese, but was always good for a joke, or shooting craps. "Want to kill some time?"

Tony's fingers felt the five dollars that would buy him a coffee and steamed bun. "Yeah, why not?"

Ah-di, a street hustler, and another guy they called Playboy, sidled up. "We in, man?"

"Yeah, you can play," Albert said.

They strolled over to the empty lot on Bayard. Tony kept one hand on the stroller, hoping Didi would sleep. The guys started pulling out their bills while Tony held back, tossing in just a buck to ante.

"Okay, Big Guy, you're the shooter," Albert said.

As Tony took the dice, Didi yelled, "*Yi yi*."

"Ha, you hear that, Tony? He says *'one one'*. Smart kid."

Tony looked at Didi and then down at the dice. "Boxcars," he whispered, "baby need new shoes." He was amazed to see the dice come to rest showing a 7 and 4. Eleven was a perfect pass and a 16 to 1 payoff.

The others groaned. *One more time, Didi,* Tony whispered. The baby looked up intently. "Wu," he gurgled. Tony thought he'd just dumped a load in his diaper — unless... *Wu* was Chinese for *five*.

He blew on the dice. "Make that five pair of shoes." The dice rolled through the air forever, the clicks explosions hitting the brick wall, then pirouetting to the pavement.

"Holy shit," Playboy said. "He did it. Five pays 30 to 1!"

"Ai-yo." Tony straightened up. "Gotta go. Penny'll kill me if I don't... Sorry guys."

Ah-di cursed in Cantonese. "You slicky boy, win my money and go home! Come back and play!"

Tony was sorry, but something had entered his life like a dragon breath. His disappointed wife loved him and their marvelous son. He would take them to dinner tonight and maybe, with his good fortune, he might even find a job as a baker pretty soon.

Too Late the Escape Plan
by Martin Shaw

1: I set my toes alight so I could see as I fell down a mineshaft.

2: When I reached the bottom there was nothing left of them to burn.

3: After using my last match to light my hair, I took a good look around.

4: There was a tunnel with a light in the distance and an old bike leant on the wall, with a hat hung on the handlebars.

5: After my hair fizzled out, I could have kicked myself!

To My Sister
by Ruth Sabath Rosenthal

I sent you an e-mail hours ago,
right after rereading a few from you,
out of the many final ones I never deleted.

According to AOL, the one I sent you today,
dated "5/30/2015 11:42:47 AM Eastern Daylight Time"
was delivered!

It's been 2 years, 1 month, 7 days, minus
approximately 9 hours, since you died
and I'm wondering if my message reached

you and, if by some miracle it did,
have you read it? I made it short, wanting
not to rehash what we've said and written

to each other since the moment we could.
Renée, if I don't hear back from you
I'll assume you can't make yourself

be heard, or choose not to. Although,
it could be I'm not listening well enough —
much the same as when you'd lived.

No matter, I'll be writing you from here
on and I'll stay on high-alert, lest I miss
a single word or whisper.

P.S. It's 3 days later and my e-mail has been returned,
unread: "Undelivered Mail Returned to Sender"
"MAILER-DAEMON," which prompted me

to look up "daemon" in the dictionary:
(in ancient Greek) archaic spelling of "demon" —
a divinity or supernatural being of nature

between gods and humans;
an inner or attendant spirit or inspiring force;
tutelary spirit; genius loci.

So, thanks to AOL, I (tend to) believe
you're out there, somewhere
in the electronic (or otherwise) universe,

perhaps, in a place universally known
as heaven. You, out there, watching me
grappling with your death 24/7.

Five Minutes
by Richard King Perkins II

I sometimes forget that my clock in the car

is set five minutes fast—

it saved me today from getting stuck in traffic

letting out from the high school

so I had that time all to myself

when I could do anything—

five minutes to write this

or not write this,

five extra minutes to do exactly something

or nothing.

Murder in Five
by Guilie Castillo Oriard

The body lies face up, the dusty ground around the head a wet brownish red. The face is gone, mostly, and what remains is coated in darkening ribbons of coagulated blood.

Gabriela's hysterics have finally subdued into—well, whatever comes after. Shock, maybe. *We're all in shock.* Staring at the body, all five of them in morbid awe of this thing they've done. This discovery that destruction is also creation.

"The shovels."

Bernice sounds odd. They all do: their voices just a little skewed, a notch down from normal. *There is no such thing as normal. Not after this.*

Annemieke gives no sign of having heard. Mayela straightens from her crouch, lets the rock drop. It falls to the ground with a gentle, all too final, thud. "I'll get them. Give me the car keys."

But Annemieke puts up a hand, as if to stop an onslaught. "We need to call someone."

Paula pauses in her improvising of a sling for Gabriela's arm. "Who?"

Annemieke looks up now, eyes wild. "Someone. We need to—"

Mayela slaps her, harder than she intended, not as hard as she deserved, but enough, with any luck, to nip panic in the bud. "We agreed. *You* agreed."

Annemieke blinks, darts a glance at the body. "He was still alive."

They all knew she, and Gabriela, would be the weaklings, the high risks. Gabriela had lost her nerve, done the deed only halfway and left the mess for the other four— for Mayela, really—to finish. But she'd done it. Terrified, with a dislocated shoulder, her fifty kilos versus his eighty-plus, she still managed to knock him out. And here Annemieke, whose only job is to fucking *drive*, is falling apart.

"I saw him breathe." Annemieke sounds like she's about to puke.

"He hurt Gaby," Mayela says, as if to a child. "We had to help. You understand that, right?"

Annemieke nods. A good sign.

"It's done now. We're back on track. And we need the shovels."

Instead of handing over the keys, Annemieke takes a step back. "I'll get them."

She disappears into the bramble and brush, but Mayela catches a glimpse of her blond hair a few meters down the slope towards the car. She seems to be running now.

Damn. "Stay here," she tells the others.

Bernice, her afro an incandescent halo back-lit against the glow of sunset, grasps Mayela's wrist. "Gaby needs a doctor."

"I know."

"If she takes the car—"

"She won't."

Mayela follows Annemieke down the slope. She doesn't need to hurry; it'll take Annemieke a while to figure out how to reconnect the car's battery.

40

*

They use the flashlights sparingly; they might be spotted from the road. Gaby, despite unimaginable pain—not just from her shoulder, but from the loss (and by her own hand, mostly) of her husband, cheat and outright cad but love of her life nonetheless—has insisted no hospital until it's done, all of it.

The faint grate of shovels in rocky soil continues long after midnight. There are, after all, two graves to dig.

Just a Digit
by Abha Iyengar

I see you staring at my right hand. Yes, there is a finger missing. I don't attempt to hide the fact. Does it take away from my charm? Do you think I am abnormal because of it? I am asking you so many questions in my mind, but you don't ask me the obvious ones. What happened? How did this happen?

As you look away, after staring at my face, my eyes, looking at how the hair curls at the nape of my neck, how the studs in my ears catch the light as the bus moves forward slowly in the mountains, I wonder if it makes a difference to you. I wonder if you will become my friend during the literary festival I know we are both attending. You look like a writer, quite a morose turn to your lips you have. Or it could be due to pity for me. Of course, I am assuming. I don't know you except I know you are interested in me.

You may be thinking, such a loss, a beautiful woman with a finger missing, something takes away from the wholeness of her, despite the fullness of her lips and the spark in her eyes. Yes, I know my plus points, have to constantly let myself know of them so I don't swing into depression. Suffered several years of it, but you would not want to know, even if we did strike up a friendship later. The seat next to me is empty and you could come sit next to me, if you liked. Perhaps this missing digit from the five required pushes you away. People look for wholeness, completeness in all things, even in a story, things must end with all the threads tied together, nothing missing.

You are a writer, you should know of people with missing parts, mostly missing a heart and a soul. This is just a digit, a number among so many. And I can use the hand very well. It took some time for adjustment. He had slammed the door shut on me, and my finger caught in the door. I was flailing my hands in the air, telling him I did not understand where he was coming from. And why he had to go. He left me in any case, with a door that shut on my hand, catching my finger. That's the story behind this new look. You would think one eventually comes to terms with losing a finger. The person can, the world cannot. See how you have looked away.

Despite all this self-talk going on in my head, wondering about you, telling you about myself, I know that very soon I will close my eyes and sleep. And if we meet at the literary festival up there in the mountains, maybe we will be friends. For writers are different, I know, and it is after all, a matter of digits, not words.

Cooking with Sue
by Mark Hudson

Yesterday was Cinco de Mayo,
and we had a celebration. Sue was the
appointed cook, and she was gracious enough
to cook, even though she had tendonitis,
and a doctor's appointment.
 She said she just got back
from Muenster, Indiana, and I said,
"Did you see any muensters?"
 And she said, "No,
but that was where the first person
in the United states diagnosed with
the MERS virus was being treated for his
condition."
 I said, "Is it contagious?
Can you get it from eating food
cooked by someone who has been
to Muenster, Indiana?"
 "No, you can't," Sue said.

Then Al said, "The worst virus you
can get is if you have an open wound
and you're swimming in Lake Michigan,
and certain viruses enter your wound
through sea slugs and things."
   And everything went
downhill from that point on.
   But nonetheless, it
was a happy Cinco de Mayo!

Round One
by Irene Buckler

Five ... four ... three ... two ... one ... go!

Though I have mentally prepared for this moment, the crush still worries me. Someone like me, who is uncomfortable in crowds, has no business being in the vanguard of such a steely-eyed surge, yet here I am. Inching ever forward, my position remains the same, relative to those with whom I am shoulder-to-shoulder. Wedged together, we are a nauseating knot of warm bodies.

As the air thickens with a heady combination of perfumes, perspiration and the lingering evidence of pungent ingested spices, I am desperate to escape and when a gap in the wall of flesh suddenly appears before me, I seize my chance. Head down, arms close by my sides, I lunge forward and break free. Others follow my lead and we start to run, but I am ahead of the pack. I know exactly where I am going and I bolt up the nearest escalator, two steps at a time.

When I eventually emerge from the Boxing Day sales, I am laden with purchases, exhausted, but happy and as I lust over my new pair of classic, red-soled, black patent leather, Christian Louboutin high-heeled shoes – a once-in-a-lifetime bargain at half price – I reflect that a little argy bargy is a small price to pay for such a prize. Roll on New Year's Day and round two!

Upfurler
by Anne E. Weisgerber

Nobody understood this could be a thing, until they saw jumpers at a certain height, five hundred eleven feet, tumble upward. Unlike fallers, upfurlers didn't make spectators jerk their shoulders in revulsion or crunch up faces to stave off crying.

Seeing upfurlers made the emergency responders slack-jawed the way a miracle can. Like if you woke up and had the 20-inch curling fingernails: it made no sense, but you'd seen pictures, and here they were. Philippe Petite kind of lay down in the air once, but this?

There was one woman in a skirt suit, hounds-tooth-checked, who spun like a saucer without rising or falling. Her hair swished behind her, swish, swish, like a sickle. They call her Frisbee now, but her name is Andrea Masterson Giacobazzi, and whatever magic, whatever science, whatever god kept spinning her like a barefoot plate, dispersed when the first tower fell, creating voids. Floor by floor boom-pancaked, boom-pancaked, and Mrs. Giacobazzi, in perfect Lagrangian coherent structures, trailed boom-boom down through the c-shaped vortices of air. Cause of death was an adult equivalent of shaken baby syndrome.

Maybe there was a level in the atmosphere where gravity recoiled in surprise that day. "It was a sweet pocket," science said, also concluding that any jumper below her event, at the unfortunate measure of 509 feet or less, fell. Mrs. Giacobazzi's children felt sadder.

Downfurlers made a horrible meaty thunking thud, then recoiled from their own private LZs, momentarily ghosted in sticky pink mists, before continuing to fall.

What was most interesting was jumpers at 511 feet and higher. They rose—tumbled and laughed and blew kisses until eventually they sensed the chill, understood they'd surpassed Everest, fell asleep, and crisped up like leaves on the way out.

From a distance, upfurlers shimmered like a murmuration, gently hovered there, like some air current snapped a soft blanket below their soft forms; their tears plocked down, but wore away to nothing before anyone could know. All science knew were puddles of blunt force trauma, cranberry and Burberry and snozzleberry and, listen. I get a little choked up thinking about it. It's that meat thock. Give me a minute. I'm not a hugger.

By family request, I cannot say more. But I'm up here. I'm up here.

Point Perfect
by Brad Garber

It was a perfect letter, five

The point, line, curve

Sensuality of prime

Alone and strong

And somewhat odd, like one

Surrounded by the sexual

Pairings of four and six

Only two removed from others

Of its kind, but in the middle.

And there, in a constant state

Of indecision, somewhere

Between reticence and recklessness

It lived a safe life, pointing

Left and right in wild

Bookish rebellion, the center

Of infinite expression.

Dark Energy with Its Foot on the Gas
by Richard Mark Glover

Stop again. Stop-stop-stop. Dominique says; "Daddy we're not moving." I grin. He grins. I walk the aisle to the bus driver – "Quisiera vamos a Isla Vieques." "Vieques?" the mustached driver says – "Hombre, how much time ju got?"

Segment one of our trip. Hitchhike (don't tell Momma, OK?) – First car stops "like whatup?" Woofers woofing. Shake of the head. "Nobody hitchhike in San Juan. Catcha gua-gua." Woofer man takes us to the stop. The people – these people, these Puerto Ricans buzzing, hot air, hot garbage, feeling this sweat, trying to help us. I mean the peeps are the blood of the land!

"How did the universe start?" Dominique asks. Five. Curious. "It's not like the A train – Harlem start, Harlem end," I say. No, I'm thinking, boy at my side, pigeons flying, rain falling. We're not in Nueva York. Astronomic skies over Ponchatoula long gone too. Waves in a Van Gogh sky. Small waves. Tiny. Infinitesimal. Motherless and loaded. Big Bang. Gotta catch that ferry – can't this thing go faster?

"Ju got two alternatives; wait for the green bus or walk Fifth Street to Sixty-fifth..." Dominique says walk. We walk. Five hundred degrees and learning new things. No.5 thing learned these people are the blood of the land! No.4 keep walking – "Hey where the Gua-gua to the Ferry at?" Dangling participle and all dangling. He short sleeved and dark sucking Marlboro say go this way that way and then that way all in PR Spanish and we see the Walgreens – this is Carolina town – cars with a/c, clocks, belle arte, here.

"The universe started with the Big Bang," I say to Dominique and he looks at me with question and I say, "That's all we got. Prevailing theory. Exploded into being. Like a nervous gun. Boom. Stars. Planets: some Mercuries, some Earths." Fortified, we walk. Dominique asks, "Why does the ferry float (and not sink)?" "By universal laws but not THE LAW (Big Bang Crazy Dark Energy with Its Foot on the Gas)." Ever-expanding. Accelerating. Walking, nearly a trot, born-again Fajardo sidewalk grandma wants to preach but we already purposed – episodes stretched out over time. Five billion years. Another car stops. "Get in." We get in. Five bucks. Five slides. "Him too?" "UH-huh." Five slide again. Blood of the land. Shotgun man turns, looks. So much can happen. Five seconds. Five years. Takes you places. Five years dark energy defined. Five years sees a lot of distance. Five minutes in a car with Mercury himself? Five more bucks. Each. "Let us out." "No". Five more bucks slide. Shotgun man now with nervous pistol. Five slide again. Five more. Eyelids red half-open half-smile half-demon eye brow quirked "THE LAW" he says – points to the pistol, mouth open, staccato laugh, five slide again, pistol waving driver driving crazy now.

Moving
by Diana J. Wynne

1. Crying the first day of kindergarten. A kindly teacher showed me a clock and wound the hands to 3:15 when it was time to go home. In a week I would be five.

2. At Saddle Rock where my mom had been the first graduating class. We'd moved back in with my grandparents. My teacher got pneumonia and never returned. In second grade a boy named David said his father had a photocopier so we decided to stage a play. My grandmother complained I gave myself the worst part in "The Princess With Rose-Colored Glasses," the angry stepmother, ignoring the fact that I directed it.

3. My grandparents had to leave the country suddenly so we rented a huge house across town. It had a burglar alarm you could set off going downstairs at night or opening the door to Western Union, sending a silent message to police. During recess at New Hyde Park Rosie ran across the schoolyard, pulling her t-shirt up over her face to flash nascent breasts. Shocked, we tried to get her to stop, never questioning why she chose this form of self-expression.

4. I loved Kensington–Johnson and Miss Lucking, a Lakers fan, and asked to be seated by her instead of with the other kids. Strangely she agreed. I had two best friends Beth and Nancy. We lived in a basement apartment with inflatable

chairs and tie-dyed jeans in the bathtub. Then my mother met Arthur, and we went to visit my grandparents in Miami. My mother bought a house but couldn't get a mover till October so I started fifth grade at K–J.

Interage was like college: lots of cozy rooms and two teachers and a big board posting all the week's activities. A lecture on the plague in Medieval England. A poetry workshop. Fourth, fifth, and sixth graders mixed together. We met individually with teachers and had music and art together but otherwise were free to read and study and sit on a sofa or the floor. It was only five weeks, the best five of my childhood, for once a classroom perfectly in tune.

5. All the previous schools were in the same town. To an adult, small adjustments. But Florida was a world away from NY and my father, though I hadn't seen him in a while, maybe years.

Bay Harbor Elementary was air-conditioned and overcrowded, days punctuated by spelling tests and current events exams. (Extra credit: # of members of Congress.) Teachers inspected my fingernails, failed my handwriting. Paddling was legal. Math was self-paced and I tore through lessons gleefully so they made me a grader one day a week. The next year I was head grader twice a week instead of learning math. I liked it well enough but where was my mother in all this?

School was my salvation, sometimes the only normal thing in my life. Something I was good at when all else failed.

Green Curl
by Neila Mezynski

Bitten bullet, breaking, taking, gagging, her dust. A girl not woman with five pointed toe. Five times five times five she bit, never once did get. It.

Odd Bird
by Jan Elman Stout

Lillian Smith had five children, all boys. "If their five each had five..." the neighbors of Davenport, Nebraska said clicking their tongues. Of course this was before Ezra was born.

Ezra was the youngest Smith. Thirteen years separated him and the oldest boy. The four older Smiths tumbled into this world one behind another. Ten years later, Ezra arrived.

"Oops," said the neighbors.

"Five's my lucky number," Miss Lillian said.

The neighbors studied Ezra, begging him to do or say what a Smith before him hadn't. That pressure could crush a lesser child, but not Ezra.

He exposed his unSmithlike talent soon enough, whistling three distinct birdcalls at the exact same time. His first combination: a warbler, a crow and a dove.

Miss Lillian told the story only one way. "When Ezra was five years old he tapped my shoulder, pursed and licked his lips and produced the most wondrous harmony of sounds."

Word of Ezra's talent crisscrossed Davenport in an hour.

"Uncanny," said the Davenport neighbors.

"It's sorcery," whispered some.

The more attention Ezra drew, the more his brothers taunted and punched him, oftentimes knocking his wind from him by thwacking his throat.

People drove through town from neighboring states to hear Ezra's birdcalls.

"Three different calls off one boy's tongue," Miss Lillian said, her bosom puffing.

"It must be a trick," the strangers said.

And so the town of Davenport voted to unearth the source of Ezra's talent.

Miss Lillian took him for a hearing test.

"A speck more acute, nothing spectacular," Mr. Ralph said, fiddling with the audiometer knobs.

His pediatrician, Dr. Tess, took the boy into her office. She poked and prodded him, palpating his organs, drawing twenty-five vials of blood, even catheterizing him and measuring his urinary output. She made an incision in his throat and clamped it open to peer inside. She found no explanation. "Vocal chords might be hyper-flexible," she said, clearing her throat.

Ezra sprang up and his talent grew with him. At thirteen, he produced five birdcalls at once, in a variety of permutations, and performed at the VFW on Saturday nights. People came from all parts to hear him, not just from Nebraska. The last couple times he performed, the audience called out every combination of trills and twitters they could think of, determined to trip him up. He moistened his lips, puckered and whistled, executing the calls perfectly each time.

At eighteen Ezra told Miss Lillian he was moving to France.

"Why?" Miss Lillian said.

Ezra shrugged. "Different birdcalls?"

"Just like that," his mother said, eyeing the suitcase in his hand.

Ezra bent, pecked her forehead.

"Good luck, son." She held the screen door open, eyes darkening as he shrank.

Weeks later, Miss Lillian received a postcard. "Dined on whole roasted ortolan. Pricked my cheek on its delicate bones. Refused to cover my head with a linen napkin. Having vocal chords severed in Rome."

At Five, Digging, I Scare Myself
by Corey Mesler

After spooning up buckets of sand
I stopped, spooked.
I swear I felt the heat from Hades.
I swear I saw the black
and yellow bodies of a million Chinese.

Knowing when to stop was an early lesson.
Still conservative in my searching
I have lost and gained equally.
I no longer fear digging too deeply
but the future is a demon
whose burning eyes I avoid like the plague.

The Windows of All Saints' Tudley
by April Bradley

Photograph, The Chancel Window, No. 8

P—

I know you remember the day we rode out to Kent, when grand house after grand house glided by. You behaved as if you were a hostage, not a guest. There were how many of us—five? Guy, James, you and me, few enough to fit comfortably in Jay's parents' Rover when he picked us up from the station in Tonbridge. It was impossible to restrain my irritation, so when Jay pointed to yet another colossus of stone (estate? palace? fortress?) I said, "It reminds me of Alcatraz." Well, it did. You know I was right. —A

Photograph, Southeast Chancel Window, No. 9

P—

The visit was dreadful. It was a tour of a perfect home whose owners went to great lengths to decorate *just so* with plaid, cabbage roses, clocks, and antique guns. We didn't appreciate his parents' extraordinary gardening skills or the

perfection of their brick pavement—now we know what a bitch it is to accomplish such bizarre, enviable perfection. They kept their wealth to themselves and spared little for their son. We had to go food shopping for him. You disliked Jay because he was uncomfortable with his poverty, whereas you had years to become accustomed to yours. Plus, he ate all our meatballs whenever we invited him over for supper. That chapped your ass like nothing else. It was cruel of you and the others when you reset all the clocks to chime at different times. He was frantic about it. I feared his father was a violent man what with all those guns and pairs of Wellingtons lined up neatly in the mudroom. Genuine Wellies. Say what you will about Jay, but he lent me his mother's boots, and at the time, the dollar was down quite a bit to the pound. I walked the Kent countryside well shod.
—A

Photograph, Gospel Aisle North Window, No. 5

P—

He gave us this remarkable thing, a story about a young woman's death and her parent's dedication of windows to a nearby church. "You must see this," Jay said. "It is unforgettable."

We walked a few miles into a field where stood the church, no one and nothing else around. The door was surprisingly unlocked. Recall how blinded we were when we ducked under the transom into a flood of lapis lazuli. It took a moment to take it all in. A few strides into the nave and we were washed in the adoring blues of Chagall's windows.

I remember your whisper, the vetiver and Tonka bean of your aftershave, the sandstone against my back, my knees perched around your hips. "Hush," you said. "Be quiet, don't let them hear you."

I never asked, the widows or the men? —A

Blind Suspicion
by Vincent Barry

The flowers were beautiful. Everyone said so. Five bunches of exquisite white petals and lustrous leafy stems. The kind of voluptuous spray that a florist would call "Sweet Remembrance" or "Bountiful Memories," perhaps "Moonlit Walk." Everyone asked about them—except Aunt Hattie.

The deceased's wife had held them under her nose and said, "Smell these, Aunt Hattie."

The guide dog looked up, then plumped his head back on the floor. Aunt Hattie inhaled deeply and sighed, "Ooh!" and "Ahh!" Then, in a smoky voice, "Musk rose."

All agreed that the flowers had a spicy, almost musky scent, and they all cantillated, "Musk rose, oh musk rose!"

They had arrived anonymously, the beautiful flowers. And everyone kept asking who sent them, who sent them, until someone said: "Aunt Hattie must have." And someone else said, "Yes, Aunt Hattie must have," and then from another, wickedly, with a curious mean pleasure: "Can you imagine—her own sister?"

Merry-go-round
by Andrew Stancek

He rips the Puddle of Mudd T-shirt and growls. "Dad, I'm not five anymore. Stop treating me like a toddler." *Then stop acting like one,* I bite down. A raging bundle of hormones at thirteen, he screamed yesterday he needed a tattoo on his face. Today he screeches a midnight curfew is totally fascist, that his mother would have allowed two a.m. at least. We throb with the knowledge that her opinion is hardly relevant since she's flown the coop for bluer skies. *A little peace, give me a little peace.*

The dress was teal and although five men swarmed around her hive, the glance was an arrow, straight to my heart. I elbowed my way in, grabbed her arm and soft-shoed us to the dance floor. Leaning into me she closed her eyes. We fused, moving in perfect union.

Targets rattle along the rutted track
Stag head
Hare tail
Carny rasps encouragement
Simon aims

Trigger finger squeezes
One-two-three-four
The fifth a miss
He mutters "shit"
Squints in dismay
Monica cackles, "Better than your father — he is all misses."

"Not all," I enfold her.

The crow on the window sill peers in, beak knocks against the glass. *No one home but us chickens*, I think. Monica is not a chicken, more a hawk. Our tradition has been to put icing and decorations on the cake together. It has cooled, cries out for pink swirls, blue rosettes. Simon's friends are about to invade. The crow squawks disdain and flies off as I pour more icing sugar into the bowl. Balloons still need to be blown up, piñata hung. I reach for the bottle under the sink, take a long pull. She wouldn't let him down on his tenth birthday, would she? The doorbell chimes and Simon scurries to the door, squeals welcome. I'm nowhere near ready. Hands shaking, I take another swig.

"It just goes to show you that you can't tell a thing about anyone."

"A little more body on the sides, a fuller look, don't you think?"

"Always seemed a nice home, even without the mother. Only two men managing, a boy and a man really, but they seemed so nice, both of them."

"Those bangs were too severe, softer will be better."

64

"When the ambulance arrived I thought a heart-attack, or a fall, had no inkling."

"Pomegranate and jasmine in this shampoo, you'll like it."

"Twenty-five stab-wounds, the radio said, dead five times over."

"You'll be the belle of the party, Marlene. That peach shade is so totally you."

"That young, he won't even go to prison, will he? Had to be insane. Joe said his arms and face were covered with blood and he bayed like a wolf as they carried him out, shackled."

Trolley Trance
by Christine Johnson

James was in Deodorants. Glancing up, he saw her – Sylvia. A glimpse, but he knew. The way she moved, golden locks flying. He dropped everything, caught her in Fruit and Veg. Pulled up short, his body millimetres from hers.

"James! It's been ages."

Graduation was a month ago.

"How're things?"

"Fine," he lied. "I'm only popping in…"

He blushed; entered that tongue-tied state Sylvia's presence provoked.

"See you then."

"No rush." He grabbed an avocado, occupied his hands. "So, what're you doing?"

"I work in Human Rights."

He gasped admiration. Exactly the Sylvia he remembered. Brave campaigner on Campus, cheeks glowing as she inspired a crowd.

"And you?"

He thought quickly. Said, "Marketing."

Her eyes drifted. "Well, must run."

Her shopping trolley wheeling past, he noticed its contents – banners and placards, petitions, flyers for justice. Then he blinked. Saw his mistake. It held nothing special, just standard Supermarket stuff.

*

Time number two, he was dawdling in Tinned Foods. Again, there, the wheaten tones of Sylvia's hair. He ducked down the next aisle, feigned surprise.

"Shopping again James?"

Sylvia's probing look unnerved him. He coughed, shuffled.

"Getting-over-flu," he mumbled.

"How's your job?"

"Great," he fabricated, "promoted. Director, Communications."

She looked at a label.

"What?"

"Nothing, congratulations," she said.

"And you?"

"Travelling, Health Centres, Third World."

"But, you don't know anything about Health – do you?"

"Decision-making for Projects, it's working with people, scoring outcomes."

She launched into detail but he half-listened, work calling.

"Let's meet, James, coffee maybe?"

As she steered past he looked into her trolley, felt dizzying awe – boxes of bandages, masses of medicines to deliver and distribute, Sylvia at the helm. Then he came to his senses. It was only olives, tampons and some salted crackers.

The next occasion he caught up with her was a day she teased him at the Checkout, telling the till-boy James was her "dearest friend" from Uni. Her words left him flushed. His frustrated eyes plumbed in wonder the glorious secrecy of her already-packed goods as she sauntered off.

Time four was a brief encounter in Frozen Goods. Sylvia was looking thin in the elegant, half-starved manner of the rich.

"Still travelling?" James asked.

"I hate travelling." Her voice was cool.

"What about those Health Centres?"

"That was ages ago."

Scanning her trolley sure of discovering new inspiration, his hopes were crushed, congealed before ice-covered things.

When he finally stumbled upon Sylvia again she'd married; a corporate lawyer. No, she wasn't working. Children? She laughed. What did he reckon?

"And you, James? Keep talking. I just need..."

They drifted past Tea & Coffee.

"I'm fine, happy," he said.

Sylvia smiled, sadly. James glanced into her trolley. This time he felt no light-headedness, there was nothing special – just a lonely bottle of tonic water and a single lime.

"Goodbye, Sylvia."

"James."

He watched her leave, stilettos clicking through Checkout, vanishing into Fine Wines and Spirits. Turning, he strode down the aisle. Supermarket Manager, until his watch said 5.00 – time for home.

I Saw the Figure 5 in Gold
by A.J. Huffman

after *I Saw the Figure 5 in Gold*, artist Charles Demuth, 1928

The corridor was black.
But blazing
with a million fires
from unseen spotlights.
Focused everywhere
except on the glass
reflecting
the infamous curve
of a figure.
Falling
first odd
then even
then odd again
until the red hours
of dawn
began to seep in
from previously unacknowledged corners.

Take Five
by Shawn Aveningo

I can name that tune
in five notes,
and by the sixth
I'm already transported.

Back to a living room circa '72,
dark walnut wood paneling,
avocado green divan.
Where Dad twirls Mom,
cutting a shag rug to a 33.

Brubeck
playing on the phonograph
so large, it takes up an entire wall.
My sister and me whirling,
ponytails swirling
to the saxophone infusion.

Our own suburban jazz club
where we *Take Five*,
a break
from the everydayness,
growing up
in middle America.

Praise the Lord and
Pass the Ammunition
by Hillary Leftwich

The women make their pies from scratch. Their hands are cracked and white with the baking flour that settles into the creases of their knuckles. They dip their fingers inside the pie filling, tasting it with the tip of their tongues. Their lips are painted red like the name on their husbands' fighter planes. *Stella Sue.*

For the past five months since their husbands left for war, they have learned to stretch and save, to make every scrap of food last. They know how to render the lard. How to trim the blood spots from the meat. The fat glistens like white gold.

Each of the women prepares coffee in early morning after their children have left for school. They take care to reuse the coffee grounds. The liquid is a dull brown and not black. It is faded like their roots.

The women's children press their hands together at suppertime, heads bowed. Their scalps are combed and clean. The women make sure of this. *Praise the Lord and pass the ammunition,* the children recite. Their smiles are innocent when their hands turn into guns. They point and shoot. You're dead, they yell.

The women miss their husbands. They eye the young men in the market as they bag their foodstuff. Sometimes they have the young men deliver their groceries to their homes. The women remove their wedding bands from their fingers and leave them on butcher blocks or kitchen windowsills. They want to feel the young men's skin, smooth as gunmetal, behind closed doors.

When the women gossip it is always about other women. How tight the flag is folded when it is passed to them, so it doesn't fall apart. They wonder when it will be their turn. They sip their coffee from bone white teacups, leaving lipstick stains on the edges. Even after scrubbing, the mark never seems to come clean.

Sometimes the women meet in sitting rooms or at kitchen tables and talk in hushed tones as their children sleep. They reminisce about school dances, football games, high school sweethearts. They rub cold cream on their chapped hands, avoiding each other's eyes. They massage the blisters on their feet, conceal their unkempt toenails. Their hair is tied up in kerchiefs, hiding their rollers. They wonder how long the curls will last the next day. They look out kitchen windows, past empty clotheslines, just beyond the town's center. They watch the night sky, uncertain. They watch as the lights from the factory blink a tired Morse code.

One Fifth
by Doug D'Elia

In Sicily lemons are the size of grapefruit.
She wanted me to know
how she took one from the tree
and cut it into five parts,
one section for each of her children

who were taught that pasta is for rich people,
be satisfied with a piece of lemon
or a cabbage or carrot, a gift
from a neighbor, boiled soft,
the juice from the pot set aside for mama.

She told me of the time a farmer
gave her an egg that she cracked
into the cast iron frying pan,
the yoke round like the sun, hot and sizzling
under a sky of stars twinkling like ten hungry eyes.

That's how it was when the kids were young,
before they were blessed with a farm of their own
and a fifth of each harvest to feed their families,
an acre set aside for neighbors, cabbages and carrots
exchanged for lemons the size of grapefruit.

Digits
by Alex Robertson

The mysteries of these phalanges
Found on limbs' end
Opposable digits the difference
Between apes and ancestors
Loping out of the forests
Grasping at straw
    harvested
In river civilisations
Apart from the Mediterranean

These neighbours
    held together
Each with a story
Like the senses
    as a part of the body

Thumb
The variance held closely
Tool handle and novel trait
The difference between successes
And not descending from the trees

Index
The pointed remark shows
A business link
    straight as the Nullarbor
Bending only to clench the hand
And something inside it

Middle
The tallest poppy in the field
Staying straight and high
The bird given with reckless abandon
A well renowned signal
    not winning any friends
A sign of wild indignation

Ring
With this finger
    I accompany thee
Over the threshold
And knots are tied in ceremony
A sense of attachment
With this metal band

Little
Made for breaking the wishbone
An extra hold to wield teacups
The smallest of the lot
But by no means the least
Together a grip for shaking

Mass Effect
by Jessica Clements

Maddie looks at my stomach and then at hers and says, "I'm so fat."

We're in my backyard, sunbaking in our bikinis. Maddie's using her elbows to prop her tiny frame up, her stomach arching inwards in a slope.

"You're not fat," I say.

Maddie looks down and pinches the skin at her belly. Last year, she was off school for a week and told everyone she'd been in a clinic for people with eating disorders. When everyone at school found out the truth – that she'd been at home crying over her dad moving out – they were still going around asking her if she was okay and making sure she'd had lunch. That's just how it is for her.

"Here," Maddie says, and hands me the bottle of canola we grabbed from the pantry. I cup my hand and pour a small puddle, sliding it over my belly until it shines. I offer it back to her but she screws up her nose. "It smells like roast," she says.

Your house smells like roast, I want to say.

We hear the front door open, the thud of my brother tossing his bag onto the living room floor.

"Let's go in," Maddie says, "I'm getting hot."

"In ten," I say.

She pokes my belly. "I'll race you," she says, grinning. "Ready? On five." She always counts to five instead of three, like it's another way for her to rebel. But before I can move she shouts "Five!" and runs to the back door.

I find her in my room, examining herself in front of my full-length mirror. Two years ago, Maddie and I were taking baths together naked, twins in our pre-pubescence.

"Have you ever made yourself sick?" she asks, running her fingertips over her ribs.

"No," I say. I close the door and stand next to her. The mirror isn't big enough for my reflection, only hers. "Have you?"

"I almost did once. It was pretty extreme."

"Maybe you should get help."

Maddie's face lights up. "Oh, I'm totally fine now! Promise."

I grab my clothes and tell Maddie I'm getting changed in my parent's en-suite. I lock myself in and stare at myself in the mirror. I think about Maddie's child-sized blue jeans sitting on my bed covers, and I wonder if I could even fit a foot inside them. I imagine what it might feel like, slipping one leg and then another into those tiny baby blues.

I find Maddie in my brother's room, sitting beside him on the bed playing *Mass Effect* on the PlayStation. She's still in her bikini, a hunch in her back making a small fold at her middle. When she sees me, she raises her eyebrows and gestures toward the door for me to leave.

I go back into my room and pick up her jeans, measuring them against my waist. I take a breath and hold them out in front of me. Ready? I say to myself. On five.

Vagabond
by Gay Degani

Her fourth school in as many grades, first grade in Florida, second, third, and fourth in California, Hawthorne, Lancaster, and now up the mountain in Mammoth, where, if she'd thought of herself as an oddball before, unused to the heat of a high desert summer, she really felt the oddball now. She blamed this newer feeling of isolation on the snow. When her father told her they were heading into the Sierras, she dreamed of snowmen with corncob pipes and snow angels carpeting an expanse of front yard. It wasn't like that at all. First off, it was cold. Icy winds slipping down the back of her neck, up her sleeves, seeping into her shoes and penetrating her gloves. And though there was plenty of smooth lovely white up above on the mountain itself, snow was dirt speckled and patchy down in the town.

And all this was bad enough, but in school it was worse. Everyone knew how to ski and that's what they did for PE, climb into a van and head four miles up the road and when all her classmates rode the lift up to the top, she was left with the kindergarteners and first graders, her too-large body awkward and prone to butt-landings, everyone standing around watching her as she struggled to get the two planks under her feet and under her. And she would sweat, her face growing red and burned from the blaze of the sun. Even the instructors laughed as they shook their heads and offered her a hand. Reluctantly she took it, knowing if they left her there, she'd freeze to death.

While they ate their chili with cut-up hot dogs, she told

78

her father she hated school, would never go again, refused to *ever* put on skis. He said, "No worries. We're moving on."

Later in bed, her homework undone, her suitcase halfway packed, she began to miss the glisten of sun on white, the smell of pine, the chubby faces of her six-year-old ski companions. Who knew what horrors she'd find in school number five.

Families of Five
by Jason Half-Pillow

I come from a family of five.

First were all the names. There were four beginning with J: Jason, Joel, Janice, and Jerry. The fifth was "Phillip". He ended up manufacturing and dealing drugs. We also had a dog named Jasper, a gratuitous and cruel gesture directed specifically at him. Maybe that explains his transition from using weed to injecting heroin.

Mom had originally been married to a man named Joe. She was from Arkansas and moved north and hid her accent, then got the man to buy a house and dumped him for my crappy soon-to-be crappy dad.

He had been married to an LSD-addled freak who had a daughter with him, and one day took off with the baby and a group of carnival cultists in an old school bus and drove the fuck off – God knows where. The girl went on to go about town everywhere on roller skates, telling dirty jokes to anyone who would listen.

Skipping ahead three decades, she was married to a cop and part of a Web-based support group almost violently advocating breastfeeding. Her cop husband's best cop friend had been shot and killed on a routine call, so she was also part of a group championing policemen's lives and calling for mandatory, no parole sentences for all cop killers – this on the breast feeding site too, near the bottom.

She was as much related to me by blood as the two half-brothers who tormented me at home – the eldest more by the general aura of soft-footed menace and never saying much; the second eldest through constant, idiot torments. Put them all together and you've got one and a half.

My half sister dated a friend of mine. He bragged to me of all the things he did to her sexually, completely unaware she was my half sister, as was, at the time, I. I found out the relation by accident and requested he kindly stop. He switched girls and gave more or less the same tiresome narrations.

He, too, came from a family of five: a Greek alcoholic father who taught him perversion; a Greek alcoholic mother who owned the only Greek restaurant in town; and two sisters – the elder respectable; the middle one, more or less a slut.

She had in common with her brother speaking always in a fake British accent. They visited their dad in London one summer and both came back cockneys. Thus did he commit to that pretense at the dumb age of 12.

Now he's 50 and visits my mother, and the two say awful things about me in their respective fake accents. Over time though, these accents have become a thing of their own. His a peculiar dialect whose origins were fake English while hers begun simply not being Southern. One shudders to think of what their kids would have sounded like.

Five Tanka
by Denny E. Marshall

wish you had a dime
every time you heard that
me, I'm not greedy
how about just a penny
for each star in universe

day of first contact
apprehension on meeting
aliens silent
not a word, left week later
after draining earths oceans

underground ice melts
forms large lakes on planet mars
thirsty crew feels like
new world sailors lost at sea
undrinkable surrounds them

never sing the song
Hank Williams, "Hey good looking,
what you got cooking."
the night you're a dinner guest
at cannibal couples house

alien message
sent to our flat screen TVs
intrudes all programs
historic while critical
vein prefer favorite show

In Crayon
by Sharon Lask Munson

Clearing out years of accumulation
she unearths her childhood drawing

family portrait of five

s
t
i
c
k

figures on green grass
wide strip of blue sky
outline of yellow sun.

Mother and father, hands clasped
as she saw them then
as she remembers them always.

Next to them, three sisters

standing in
     g
      r
       a
        d
        u
       a
      t
      e
     d
          order

her right arm around the youngest
same pose she recognizes
from decades of black and white snapshots

elder sister
one giant step to the left
               face turned

     shadowed by a colossal elm

         even as a child   a solitary figure.

We Called Her Mrs. H.
by Joanne Jagoda

I can't smell Chanel No. 5 without remembering her, though it's been more than fifty years. We called her Mrs. H. because her last name was Russian and difficult to pronounce. Her perfume preceded her up the steps to our house like a magic genie wafting through the front door, announcing her arrival even before she rang the bell. It was my mother who told us it was Chanel, because we didn't know one perfume from another. To us it smelled strong and exotic.

Wednesday afternoons she would come for our piano lessons. My sister had considerable musical ability, but I was hopeless and never practiced. That didn't matter to her because Mrs. H needed the $7.50 my mother paid for our lessons.

We were mesmerized when she disrobed, doffing her green high-collared wool coat. Then pulling off her black kid gloves one at a time, uncoiling her lace scarf, powdering her nose from a compact, and removing her pillbox hat. She placed her clothes neatly on the edge of our gold brocade sofa. Mrs. H. had arrived from Russia years before, a fifth cousin of some relative of the Czar and still spoke English with a heavy Russian accent. She was elegant and regal, and we pretended she used to be a princess. Maybe that wasn't so far from the truth, but sadly she eked out a living teaching piano.

I hid behind the dining room door, praying she would forget about my lesson, but she never did. Her metronome tick-ticking on top of the piano, when I stumbled over the scales or the simple pieces, she leaned over, "tsked-tsked" and patiently modeled how to do them, graceful fingers flying over the keys.

After the lessons when my mother asked how we did, her standard answer was, "the girls are so ny-us, so ny-us" meaning we were *nice* but said nothing about our musical talent. My mother offered her hot tea and homemade butter cookies which she gratefully accepted before she went on to catch the public bus to get to her next lesson.

We loved to sit close to her, listening to her stories about Russia and how her family lived before the revolution. One afternoon we found out her late husband gave her Chanel No. 5 for her birthdays, and she wore it every day in his memory.

When she stood to leave, she pulled on her coat, gloves, and lace scarf. Then came the best part. My mother handed her the $7.50, and carefully unzipping the lining of her pillbox hat, she stashed the money inside. She had been robbed once by "hooligans" and could not take the chance of having her purse grabbed again.

When she admonished us to practice harder, we dutifully nodded and smiled crossing our fingers behind our backs. We watched as she clutched her purse with one hand and with the other gripped the iron railing shuffling down the steps.

Chanel No. 5 lingered long after and forever in my memory.

The List His Wife Left
by Gwendolyn Joyce Mintz

Her voice is a sweet whisper in his ear. "You need to get it done," she tells him. Adds "*today*," though that word is not coated. He knows she's frustrated.

Face scrunched against the pillow, he mumbles, "As soon as I get up."

She smiles as if she believes him – she wants to believe him – but he's promised the same thing the day before and several before that.

Now that he's back, she wants him to take responsibility, to make decisions, execute some plans. "I'm tired of carrying it all," she's said. "I need your help."

When she's gone to her job, he rises, sits on the side of the bed. From the nightstand, he picks up the piece of paper. He scans it. Still the same tasks she's been asking him to do. It's only five things but he can't find the energy to figure out how to do one.

His hands tremble and his breath quickens. The paper falls to the floor. Elbows on his knees, his face lowers into his hands. He breathes deep.

Being home is worry and problems. War had been easy. To do: Don't die.

Nighttime in Sicily
by Townsend Walker

The cat had a fish clamped in its mouth. Before the fish ceased to wriggle the cat's head was severed from its body and placed on the mantle. Fausto stepped back from the tableau to appraise the effect. The light behind him was so bright, so crystalline as it shone through the window, that it took up part of the room, became a palpable physical presence. That often happened this time of year in Siracusa, in the late afternoon, near five o'clock, shortly before the sirocco dominated the city. He was compelled to move to the doorway to obtain an unfettered view of the tabby cat head and silvery fish.

"I think that works," he said to himself. "Camille, come look. Do you think that will make your mother happy?"

"Without question. Why do you ask? You know Mother never liked fish."

The phone in the hallway rang. Fausto picked up.

"Giuseppe, come stai? No, nothing at all. We're sitting around enjoying a lazy afternoon by the pool."

"Not this evening, Camille's mother is coming to dinner. Another time? Si. Ciao."

"Why did you tell him Mother was coming over?"

"I didn't want him to know I was meeting with Salvo."

"You are?"

"We have business to attend to this evening."

"Be careful, caro."

*

At nightfall, Fausto met Salvo at a café in Piazza di Duomo. A full moon bounced off the white marble paving, illuminating the square. They hurried into a small black car waiting in via Cavour.

"He will be there? Alone?"

"He thinks he is meeting the Santini boys."

They rode in the cramped silence of the tiny Fiat 500. As they approached the Amphitheater they saw a lone figure standing by a streetlight. The car stopped, the two men opened their doors.

"Il Gatto?"

"Si."

Salvo pulled the revolver from his pocket and fired. Fausto pulled the fish from his pocket and put it in the mouth of Il Gatto.

Those who try to swallow a fish in one bite often go hungry. Nor do they drink the new wine.

Theory of Numbers
by Lori Gravley

Five is the set of all possible numbers that each
have five members.

Principia Mathmatica, Russell and Whitehead

Each day I count for you—your one body,

one step, one more night without sleep, your one mouth

you've learned to bring close. Two sucks,

two weeks since I washed the floors,

two steps my fingers take to find the spot beneath your chin,

your two eyes wide and laughing. Three little pigs,

three bears, three months since I've seen

a movie or sat alone through a whole meal, three

billy goats gruff, thirty minutes to write a poem

while you nap. No more than four ounces of juice a day,

four changed diapers, and every time

I count your five little toes, you learn to number your days,

the hours in and out of bed and all the minutes

you must wait until I lift you up and dance again.

Photographic Memory
by Susan Tally

When my stepmother extended

Her proud hand around

My reticent shoulder,

It was the vulnerability

In her heated palm

And fingers that reminded me

To think about what it is like

To be seventy-five

That hot day

In Florida

When we posed together.

Five to One
by Michael Webb

I walk in, past the front desk, and over to the elevator. I can hear a radio playing faintly, and I can make out the organ and the drum signature of a Doors song. I make eye contact with the girl behind the desk, a trim African American girl with her hair blown out into a mass of brown curls. Visitors are supposed to check in at the desk, but she knows my face, and she nods permission at me while she continues her conversation. She knows where I am going. I half turn so I can continue looking at her as the elevator arrives. I can see the firm curves of her hips under tight jeans, the uniform polo shirt she wears tucked in tight. She leaves little to the imagination.

The elevator doors open and I ride up alone. I try to place the song I had heard, the thumping, lumbering beat, and after a second, the doors open and I remember it. "Five To One". I turn into Stephen's room, and the familiar sights assault me. The bed, the rails, his skin ghostly and thin over his proud cheekbones, his body bony and wasted. The machines, purring and wheezing, the display of his heart rate and respirations and blood pressure, the numbers bright and clear against the dark displays. The light over his bed is off, and I don't bother turning it on.

I always talk to him, and every time I do, I feel foolish. But I relate my day to him, student conferences and classes and a conversation about Ulysses with an English professor who I suspect has had designs on me. I talk about the draft in the upstairs hall I'm finally going to have someone look at, and the consideration I've been giving to selling our second car.

He doesn't respond, but, of course, he never does, since a stroke last November left him functionally a house plant, capable of eating through a tube and excreting through another but no speech, no life, no spark, no sign of the man I married the summer Jim Morrison died. I tell him about the song I heard, about the girl with the huge hair, I remind him how I will always associate that song with our crappy Allston apartment and the hot days we spent on our mattress, tangled in sweat and lust and one another.

I watch my husband's chest rise and fall, trying to connect the shell on the bed with my Stephen, young and strong and bearded, fucking me hard on the floor with the Doors playing above our heads, a framed magazine cover with Morrison's face hanging on the wall, watching us as we do it, a leer on his face. I think about the girl downstairs, and I hope she has someone who will give her memories that almost make up for the aching loneliness of now.

Crib Sheets
by Annabelle Baptista

When I arrived, the first day, people surrounded me on all sides – oohing. I made a mental note of smiling, warm words and kisses as needful things. I saw bright lights and heard people talking, hushed. By comparison, home sounded like a tear-gassed riot. A chief and her medicine man managed the natives, my five siblings: my tribe.

At eleven months old, possibly due to the tribe's food scarcity, my brothers left me at the park. Fortunately, it was summer. Once the chief picked me up; I grabbed her hair – ranting in babble – what were my chances of survival among the y!oungs. She told the medicine man, "Put her in her crib! Put her back!"

However, I knew he couldn't put me back – no magic could – even I knew that teepee was closed. That night, hearing the drums and smelling smoke, setters came, littered my crib with their wraps and skins, and as no-matter setters – settled in.

I adapted, grew, and by my second year, I had learned to hold on tight when someone swung me by my arms, or pray, when tossed in the air. I learned – for a girl – I had a hard head.

My weapon for years was my tears. Weeping sheets of saline solution seemed to penetrate indifference and conceivably alter behavior. The tribe named me cry-baby-in-wet-pants. I hunted with the dogs that followed the tribe, ate their food, and questioned the Shepherd, why they stayed — "For keep and safety," he said.

I learned hair was important; mine hot combed and greased garnished admirable looks as I flopped around all weekend on someone's hip like a shrunken head.

My eldest sister Leta was deaf, arson, in an abandoned building, third degree burns. I trusted her more than I trusted the others — who seemed to have a casual regard for my safety. She smiled a lot at me, and one day I was speaking nonsense and when I turned my head, she stabbed me. Shocked — I let out a ratcheted scream, my eyes and nose viscous geysers fed by pain. Leta tried to cheer and cajole me. It wasn't until my sister Carla came in the room and enunciated, "You pinned her to her diaper," that I understood. Luckily, I didn't bleed much.

The Chief and her Medicine man's rituals were as follows: they lived in bed. They smoked, slept, and ate there while watching TV and enjoying inhalable powder or the Medicine man's pipe.

I learned we were not hunters, but transient gatherers of detritus which we try to turn into money — alchemists perhaps? Further study is required.

I'll be six this year, able to leave the house for an eight-hour day. Unfortunately, I've learned kindergarteners are unpaid labor. They say the education system is a maze; not everyone finds their way, but you should stay in it until you find an unsubstantiated artifact called a dream — which you keep or lose, in an arena called — a mall.

Alphanumeric XYZV>5
by Daniel Y. Harris

Input is *x*. Output is *y*. The set is *z*. The manifold is *v*.
We have reached the regressand and minimize game
for alphanumeric logins, oiled in these focus-killing
television shows. Five-eye drills blind to a vacant
blur, gorging on binaries and pissed at the solution.
How long past rock blood was he supposed to live?
Long enough to curl density and be buried in grime.
The mulberry's lobed shoots turn dark purple: ripen,
drop and mix with Chicago dirt. Rat holes multiply.
Entropy is a rotted log, mounted like a pagan god
against a pink and grey chipped garage. The ashes
of dead parents are white-fruited cultivars. Eddy's
on the brink of fertility and new abs. Mind control
is dead. He exercises the lot and makes no claims.

Love in Five Steps
by Allison Sobczak

One

He makes a strong impression by spilling his hazelnut coffee down the front of her black pencil skirt. With a gasp, she launches off the seat just as he bends down to help wipe up the mess. Knee collides with nose, and later, when the blood flow slows and the burn begins to fade, she agrees to his treat of a second cup of coffee.

Two

While he would've suffered through a rom-com, he's happy to learn that she's just as excited to see the newly-released horror schlock as much as he is. He buys two tickets and texts her with the tale that his friend just bailed and now he's stuck with an extra and would she like to join him? She accepts with a smiley face emoji.

Three

He finds her standing in front of a cage that houses a caramel-colored English bulldog puppy, its wet, wrinkly snout snuffling at the cage door. She squats and presses her fingers to the bars, letting the puppy lick them. She turns to look up at him pleadingly. Later, after they've bought the dog bed and the chew toys and the leashes and the collar and Hank the puppy is exploring the apartment's entrance hallway, she puts her arms around his neck and kisses "Thank you" into his skin.

Four

He takes her to the highest viewpoint of Mount Rainier and proposes to her among the frosty tree branches and snowy fields. His knee is soaked through and numb from where he kneels, but it bothers him less and less the more and more she smiles and laughs and cries "Yes, yes, yes! Of course! Yes!"

Five

She's a vision in her ivory gown and lace veil, walking down the aisle on her father's arm. She continually shifts her gaze from his eyes to their clasped hands while the priest begins his speech about love, unity, and togetherness. When the vows and rings and "I do"s have been exchanged, he finally kisses his wife. She tastes like hazelnut.

Later, many years later, when he thinks back on this moment, he realizes how stiff her lips felt against his, how her smile didn't crinkle at the corners, and how the sheen in her eyes told a story without a happy ending.

Weeds of the World (Unite!)
by Darryl Price

We invade the invaders and they invade us, these little
Blooming weeds. They raise five flowers and let them blow
Into the winds like fleets of stars. All of us
Steer by their turning tide. All of us will eventually
Fall by their shining example into wintry skies, crisp and

Dispersing everywhere like snow, but they do not give up
That ghost. Instead they regrow even the frozen toes of
Heaven into an eruption of abundant walking shoes, the kind
To take you wherever you are going, and with whom.
This is the miracle of green life. It exists solely

To exist. It will not take no for an answer.
It sucks sunshine like it's going out of style and
Spits it back out in puffs of pure oxygenated cookies,
Baked to perfection and ready to eat. And once inside
Of your guts it works its ancient magical spell like

Clockwork, restoring even the most cynical nature back to its
Original joy in simply breathing again. And then of course
Comes another blast on the field from all the trumpets
At hand to signal the war is not yet over
For some of us, we must go on to the

Gates of forever, some alone and some of us together.
At either end the greening will take its rightful place
In the conversation about the meaning of all love within
The meaning of all life. And because of that this
Poem finds its way to you today, making so sure.

My Princess
by Matt DeVirgiliis

Fernando shifted in his metal chair, waiting for the immigration agent to talk. So, the agent said, you'd like to stay?

Si, signore, said Fernando. Ah, yes.

What does Orlando have that Naples doesn't?

We have the best wine in the world. We have beaches and an old-world feel. And my family is there.

But?

But, continued Fernando, it was my fifth day on the job at the Italian restaurant in Epcot. We're a squirrelly bunch. Everyone's from different regions of Italy and all excited to be here – just as excited as the tourists. And we're making money. More than I could at home. They even give us free admission to the parks. We can walk around, go on rides, and get our picture taken in front of Cinderella's castle.

You're having a good time.

Ah, sir, that's not all of it. Or how do I say it?

The best is yet to come.

Yes, yes.

The agent closed the manila folder on his desk and pushed it aside. He smiled.

You know something I do not? asked Fernando.

Keep going.

Fernando sat back in his chair. He looked at Agent Parker. Well groomed. Comfortable. Tie loose and sleeves rolled. But he nervously twisted his gold wedding band with his opposite hand. Agent Parker nodded his head… waiting.

It was my fifth day on the job. Before my shift, we went to Magic Kingdom to explore. I met the group at the entrance and there she was, standing with the rest. Her name is Abilene. The visitors say that place is magical. They like the shows, the costumes, and they feel good. She made it magical that day.

Agent Parker chuckled.

The sun – it's big here – lit up her black hair. Her skin was like smooth chocolate. Her green eyes glimmered like fireflies. But it was her smile. Her nose crinkled. Not a wrinkle. A crinkle, you see.

We did everything that day – It's a Small World, Peter Pan, and Haunted Mansion. Then they set off the fireworks over Cinderella's castle. We shared cotton candy. She smiled every time I handed it back to her and I saw that crinkle.

You met someone.

I met my princess.

How long do you want to stay?

As long as she is here.

Agent Parker picked up a picture frame that lay facedown on his desk, stood it upright, and grinned. Congratulations, Fernando, he said and extended his right hand.

Fernando shook Parker's hand excitedly. Thank you, signore. That place is magical.

I'll extend you as long as possible. Take care of the paper work today.

Thank you, sir.

Thank you, Fernando.

Fernando ran out of the office. Parker picked up his phone and dialed. Hello, a woman said.

Hi, honey. I'm sorry about what I said this morning. I have an idea for our anniversary.

Let Them Eat Cock
by Stephen V. Ramey

Seemingly overnight, Maggie McGee has become the world's biggest porn sensation. At 500 pounds, she's always been the biggest porn star, but now she's also the highest grossing, with five features scheduled to release this month alone. She's not a beautiful woman, but porn has never really been about beauty. Attitude matters more. And that, Maggie McGee has in spades.

It's her signature move—known in the industry as the red shower—that launched her. Legend has it that she discovered it by accident. Some poor sod of a stunt double mistook a yawn for an invitation and she bit his penis off. One story goes that he was rushed to a hospital to have it reattached, but I know a lighting guy who insists she swallowed. I'm inclined to believe him, given Maggie's reputation.

In any case, she was on to something and the producers knew it. Her next film, *The White Widow*, saw three manhoods chomped. Quick cuts made it clear that she wasn't actually eating those dicks, but the blood was convincing.

Even that extreme was not extreme enough for long. Soon Maggie was flaunting fresh-severed wieners, drinking bloody Marty's, hosting bondage barbecues in foreskin boots. The tabloids took notice.

Up and coming male stars appeared on Maggie's arm. It became a badge of honor to "survive" a night with her. She played along, but you could tell she was bored when an

105

action star bragged he had endured an intimate encounter. "Bite it?" she reportedly quipped, "I couldn't even find it."

All in good fun, right? Not really. Can you imagine the suffering those men endure, the humiliation? They're paid well, but for most it's a one-time gig. Why do they do it?

Which brings me to this: I have been cast for a vid that has Maggie blasting through scenes in a Marie Antoinette wig, wielding a miniature guillotine in inventive ways. She barges into a hot dog eating contest only, of course, her dogs are penises severed from men from the audience.

The script calls for one of us to emerge intact. Maggie will choose the lucky fellow based upon performance. My agent says it's the opportunity of a lifetime; I'm the best money shot there's ever been.

I try to imagine Maggie's plump finger pressing the release, that blade jamming above my fast-wilting flesh. *You have been spared!* But I wonder if my time has come, longing has replaced good sense, if maybe deep down we don't all share a death wish. We take this journey to be worshipped, and there comes a time when we will do *anything* to stand in that spotlight.

In my thoughts, the blade continues, blood spurts across Maggie's cheek, her eyes edge wide, her smile. And a five-inch segment of flaccid penis, my badge of honor, flies from her hand to the ravenous crowd.

Will they cheer?

Togetherness
by Matt Potter

Pink. Purple. Blue. Green. *Yellow?*

Anxiety. Insomnia. Back Pain. Depression. _____?

Mum clunks the glass of water on the table, beside the tablets lined across the laminex.

"Down the hatch, darling," she says, wiping her hands down her apron. "Let's not make a fuss."

Yellow?

Why has four become five?

"What's the yellow one for?" I ask.

"It's just another pill, dear."

Mum runs her blotchy hands across her face, dropping them into the pockets on her apron. Shoulders sagging, she turns away towards the sink.

"The doctor prescribed it for you," she says. "To help you lose weight."

I pick the yellow pill up with my fingers. It's dusty, probably from the emery board Mum used to rub away the skull and crossbones.

"If you want to get a job, and earn money, and rejoin the world, you've got to lose some weight first so you can fit through the front door."

The tips of my fingers are covered with yellow powder.

"Just swallow the damn thing, Christopher!!"

I put the pill in my mouth, sip water from the glass, and swallow.

Mum turns, a smile across her face. "That wasn't too hard now, was it?"

I pick up the green pill, working my way down the line, just like I'm expected to.

Bitch.

Slammer
by Phillis Ideal

"Please, please grant me probation and a deferred sentence with no time behind these walls. I have never had a driving ticket before. NOW one Margarita and a DUI. Never again!"

Five in the afternoon was the magic hour that six male prisoners and I were to be checked out and released.

A guard who was seven feet tall and three times as wide as any doorway gave me a bag of my clothes and an opaque sealed package, which contained my ID, jewelry, wallet and cell phone. He told me to change out of my green jail scrubs into my street clothes and to sign off that I had all my belongings. It was impossible to see through the plastic so I asked if he would open it for me.

He inhaled deeply, showing off his huge chest heaving with power, and stood within a few inches of me. His voice had the shattering force of a wrecking ball. *"You sign off that you have all of your items and then you go out that door. You will not be allowed back in."*

Startled, I tilted my head to meet his hostile glare. He was the strongman of the snake world, a boa constrictor wrapping around its victim. Terror began squeezing the life out of me: I couldn't breathe and my heart pounded. I scrawled my signature and scrambled out the one-way exit door to the street. The lock on the door clicked behind me.

Out in the parking lot with a dead phone, no sign of transportation, and a ten-mile walk to the city, I wondered if

I would make it home. I rummaged through my wallet, found my credit cards but saw that $70 was stolen. I didn't have five cents on me. I was alone and stranded. I fought back tears as I frantically walked in circles, and then stopped to stare at the ground, as if I were about to float away. Just as I was walking in the direction of the highway, a municipal bus slowly pulled into the parking lot. I sat in a seat across from the bus driver.

"I have no money but need to get to town. Where is your first stop?"

"This is a municipal bus and there is no charge," she said. "The next stop in town is at the mall and you can get off there."

"May I use your phone to call my friend to pick me up?" She handed it to me with a smile. I had forgotten about gestures of kindness. The bus dropped me off at the shopping center where my friend met me with a large bouquet of sunflowers. I had only seen three or four drab colors and touched only concrete and steel for what seemed an eternity.

The bright yellow of the flowers dazzled and overwhelmed me.

I slipped on my sunglasses.

Jailhouse Jive
by Peter DiChellis

Howie and Wheezy had landed in jail again, this time on a second-degree daytime burglary bust. The central holding cell stank of fresh sweat and stale b.o., and buzzed with a cacophony of malevolent hoots and timid sobs.

Wheezy surveyed the mayhem. "I ain't built for jail," he said. "And I still owe the bail man money from last month."

"No troubles," Howie said. "I seen an ad for some lawyer fellas on TV. Easy name to remember too. Johnson, Johnson, Johnson, Johnson, and Johnson. Call 1-800 Johnson."

"Five of 'em? A lot of damn Johnsons."

"Lawyers, ain't they? I'll use my jailhouse phone call to get us one, and you use your call and fix us with some money."

A beefy guard with tired eyes and a jowly face escorted the two prisoners to the jailhouse phone. "Local only. Ten minutes," he told them. He backed up a few steps.

A spit-speckled black phone waited, bolted to a scarred metal table. Howie punched in the lawyers' 1-800 number while Wheezy stood beside him.

A man answered, his deep voice pure business. "Johnson, Johnson, Johnson, Johnson, and Johnson."

Howie gave Wheezy a thumbs-up. "I need to talk to Mr. Johnson," he said into the phone. "It's real bad."

"I'm very sorry, but he's in court today."

Howie put his hand over the phone's mouthpiece and

111

looked at Wheezy. "Ain't there."

"Ask for another one," Wheezy said.

Howie spoke into the phone again. "Then I'll talk to Mr. Johnson instead."

"I'm afraid he's on vacation this week."

Howie glanced at Wheezy and shook his head.

"Get another one!" Wheezy hollered.

"Well then, I guess I'll talk to Mr. Johnson," Howie said.

"I'm terribly sorry, but he's no longer with the firm."

Howie shook his head again.

Wheezy's bloodshot eyes bugged out like painted Easter eggs. "Get somebody!" he yowled.

"How about Mr. Johnson?" Howie said into the phone.

"No. He's in a meeting and can't be disturbed."

Howie put his hand over the mouthpiece and spoke to Wheezy again. "Him neither!"

"Get somebody! Get somebody! I can't stay in jail!"

"What about Mr. Johnson?" Howie asked the man on the phone.

"This is Mr. Johnson speaking. How may I help you?"

Howie turned to Wheezy, beaming this time. "Okay!" he said. "I got Mr. Johnson now."

Speed Dating for Widows
by Helia Rethmann

"What I like best about these events is their efficiency," the widow said.

"Efficiency, yes, yes, exactly right," agreed the suitor.

"No time wasted dancing around," the widow said.

"No time wasted," the suitor agreed. In truth, he missed the dancing.

"Tell me five things you're looking for," the widow said.

"Of course. Yes. I…ah…admire large females."

"Good. Proceed," the widow said.

"And, well – I am rather romantic."

"Romantic as in 'would give a body part for'–?" the widow inquired.

"If need be." The suitor swallowed.

"Go on," the widow said.

"I like your hourglass figure."

The widow sighed and examined her pincers.

"Sorry," the suitor said, "It's just… nerves, I guess. I appreciate females who don't focus on size."

"Not a problem," the widow said. He was very much on the small side, she had noted, but liked him better for it. "And five?"

"You seem so…assertive, and I … I … I am …–"

"Timid? Cautious? Shy?" the widow prompted.

The suitor nodded.

They were silent while she made her decision.

Finally, she held out her hairy arms.

"You may approach," she said.

The suitor blinked. He moved hesitantly at first, then with more confidence, as he came to rest against her.

"Isn't this nice?" the widow said, after a while.

"Much nicer than I imagined it to be," the suitor said.

His voice was high-pitched and, the widow noticed, his eyes were bulging.

"It's even better with your eyes closed," she said.

When he closed his eyes, she ate him.

Building a secure home would take time, but the first step was taken, and she felt renewed energy.

"Much easier than I imagined it to be," she said, to no-one in particular.

Five Men and My Tits
by Shannon Coghlan Reiss

I have fake tits. The way I see it, I earned them. Before my plastic surgeon opened me up and stuffed me full of saline, I was a 32 double-A. That's so flat even strangers stopped me to say, "You're so flat."

I nursed my youngest son until he was eighteen months old. I remember the sensation of milk filling my breasts and the tingle of its release. I remember the sound of little gulps, the look of satisfaction on a chubby baby face.

I stopped breastfeeding because I wanted to have sex with a boy who was seven years younger than me, who didn't know I was nursing, but did know I was married. He loved my small tits. Six months after that, I wasn't married anymore.

After my ex-husband ran off to Alaska or Las Vegas or wherever he ran off to, I worked nine hours a day at a telemarketing job and smoked cigarettes on my breaks. I ran twelve miles every Saturday. I forgot what it was like to feel a man's breath on my nipples.

When I told my mom I wanted a boob job, she stopped talking to me. Afterwards, she admitted they looked natural and then she talked to me again.

A month after my surgery, I fell in love with a Marine sniper who killed Iraqis. He loved my fake tits. When the sniper got tired of me, I moved onto an air marshal who never killed anybody. He loved my fake tits too. He proposed to me and I declined. He proposed to me again and I accepted knowing I wouldn't marry him.

A few years later, I did get married. Not to the young boy or the sniper or the air marshal. My husband loves my tits more than any of them ever did. He loves my tits because they're mine, not because I'm a 34 double-D. He would love my tits if they were flat, although I suspect he loves them more the way they are now. But trust me, he would still love my tits.

In a couple of years, these implants will have to be replaced. That makes me sad, because we've been through so much together.

Happy Again
by Mandy Nicol

Joe had dreamed the same dream for five nights and in the morning, after each dream, he pored over the form guide looking for a grey horse with a yellow-silked jockey.

On Saturday morning he found it.

"I found it!" he shouted, so suddenly that his wife spilled her bowl of Weet-Bix over the kitchen table. Joe stabbed his finger at the paper several times. "Number five in race five, grey colt, jockey's colours all yellow. It's called Happy Again." He beamed a nicotine smile at Bev. "This is the horse I've been dreaming about luv, the one that'll win us a fortune. Better find your hat, we're off to Flemington."

Bev didn't wear a hat, after all this wasn't the Melbourne Cup, but she did wear her good red pantsuit. And a yellow scarf, for luck.

As the horses cantered to the start for the fifth race Joe and Bev found seats in the grandstand. Joe fixed his binoculars on Happy Again while Bev gripped the betting ticket with both hands. Five hundred dollars gambled on a dream. Joe was mad, stark raving mad.

"Five hundred dollars is such a lot of money, Joe," she said. Not for the first time.

"It had to be five or five hundred luv, I couldn't ignore all those fives. Number five in race five, drawn barrier five, at five to one odds." He shrugged his shoulders. "That's gotta mean something."

"Maybe it means he'll run fifth," Bev said slowly.

Joe lowered his binoculars and turned to her. "Hell," he said. "I didn't think of that."

But Happy Again didn't run fifth.

He ran second last.

The grandstand emptied around them. Neither said a word. Bev folded the betting ticket in two and tucked it away in her purse. They shuffled to the bar in silence.

Bev sipped her gin and tonic and scanned the form guide. "I've found a horse in the next," she announced.

Joe gulped his beer.

"I think it's your dream horse," Bev added.

Joe banged his glass on the table and snatched the form guide. "I didn't see a grey in it."

"I don't know what colour the horse is, but it's number seventeen. Daffodil Skies."

Joe looked at the paper and screwed up his nose. "And how's that my dream horse?"

"Well, daffodils are yellow, and..." Bev paused dramatically, "...the jockey is P. Winter."

"So what?"

"Winter skies are grey."

Joe finished his beer. "Sounds bloody convoluted to me luv," he said. "And anyway, it's got no chance. It's a hundred to one."

*

Bev gripped the betting ticket with both hands.

"I don't believe it. I don't bloody believe it," said Joe. Not for the first time. "Five bucks on the nose of a hundred to one shot and it romps home. You know what Bev? You've gone and won back all that I lost."

"Yes," grinned Bev. "I know."

And she carefully folded the betting ticket in two and tucked it away in her purse.

Post and Beam
by Barbara Ruth

I had no idea what post and beam construction was, and I'm still pretty hazy on the specifics. But in 1975 the amazonian women I was meeting knew how to do it, and were teaching it to others. I had become co-coordinator of the Free Women's School five months before I visited my parents, between the first Michigan Womyn's Music Festival and the National Radical Feminist Conference, both in August of that year. My father laughed when I showed him the brochure about FWS. "Auto Repair? Self-defence? You don't know anything about that. Are you going to be the teacher?" he smirked.

"No," I told him. "But I know how to find women who can teach all of the things the FWS offers." I had no doubts whatsoever that I could find a woman to teach any skill or facilitate a study group on any subject Philly sisters wanted to learn. Not because I was such a great resource finder, but because lesbian feminists were reinventing the world: our wisdom deep, our number legion. Sandwiched between being on the land at Michigan, and then again at NRFC, Dad's version of How Things Are didn't stand a chance.

Spring Break
by Paul Beckman

We were five couples, all long out of college in St. Thomas on Spring Break while our kids were Spring Breaking it in Cancun.

Nursing a hangover on our second day we went to the beach and for breakfast ordered nachos and margaritas. After a couple of eye-openers we carried our third one into the water and cooled off and chatted.

Mirsky, barefoot, steps on a sea urchin, starts screaming and drops his margarita. The rest of us were wearing water shoes so we help him back up on the beach and someone says the only cure for the sting is urine and we get to talking about which one of us guys is going to pee on Mirsky's foot.

The wives want in on the action and a discussion on the ability of women to aim pursues and they go all defensive on us so we say what the hey they can join in and meanwhile we're feeding Mirsky more margaritas to keep him quiet.

No one thinks to call the resort nurse or doctor but we do decide to have a backgammon tournament and the winner gets to pee on Mirsky. Even Elaine, his wife, wants in on this.

We've attracted a bit of attention with our raucous behavior and it's turning out to be like a car wreck on I-95 going the opposite direction. Rubberneckers abound. Finally, someone suggests we check on Mirsky. We look over from our backgammon tournament and he's laying where we left him in the sand but there's a man with three kids peeing on him. We leave our games and walk over, pissed that someone is doing our job for our buddy. The youngest kid, about six, is peeing on Mirsky's knee while the father and his two teenage sons are whizzing on the foot in just the right spot.

They finish, some of us get on their case for butting in, and Mirsky thanks them and says his pain is gone and then he tells them what great friends they are. Mirsky's attitude shows that he's gone over to the other side so we huddle and walk away leaving him at the water's edge as the tide rolls in.

Five Boxes of Pornography
by Sally Reno

From the shoeboxes we found in his closet, it seemed he had once sold porn to the Navy boys. Picture a teenaged Abelardo, skinny, not too tall, slinking through the Navy bars on stacked heels, with packets of pornographic photos and another packet of Cuban cigars in his zoot suit, and a wad of cash.

It looked like he was out of that business by the end of WWII. That would have been when he began to make it big as a Latin dancer. The WWII era porn was glossy and unpleasant but the WWI stuff was... frankly challenging: brutish looking Pistol Petes with licorice-whip mustaches and girls with rolled stockings and physiques like pools of tallow were doing things in sepia with parlor furniture and each other that clearly did not interest any of them in the slightest. They stared straight at the camera with a look that said, "So?"

Authors

Alex Reece Abbott

writes across genres, forms and hemispheres. Regularly published here and there, including in *Landmarks: the 2015 National Flash-Fiction Day Anthology*, her short fiction has won the Northern Crime Competition and the Arvon Prize and often shortlists, including for the Bridport Prize, Fish, Mslexia and Lorian Hemingway. A *writing.ie Short Story of the Year* nominee, her novel, *Last of the Lucky Country*, shortlisted for the 2015 Northern Crime Competition.

Shawn Aveningo

is an award-winning, globally-published poet whose work has appeared in over 80 literary journals and anthologies, including LA's *poeticdiversity* who recently nominated her poetry for a Pushcart Prize. She is co-founder of *The Poetry Box®* (www.thepoetrybox.com), managing editor of *The Poeming Pigeon* and journal designer for *VoiceCatcher*. Shawn is a proud mother of three and shares in the creative life with her husband in Beaverton, Oregon.

Annabelle Baptista

is a poet and short story writer born in Indianapolis, Indiana. She currently teaches English as a second language and lives near Heidelberg, Germany with her husband. She has been published in *Coloring Book: An Eclectic Collection of Fiction and Poetry, andwerve* and *Families: The Front Line of Pluralism*.

Vincent Barry

has authored (or co-authored) numerous philosophy texts. His fiction has appeared in various journals in the United States: *Writing Tomorrow Magazine*, *The Write Room*, *Blue Lake Review*, *Crack the Spine*, *The Vignette Review*, *BULL*. Earlier in his career, Barry had one-act plays produced at New York's American Place Theatre and had a residency at the Edward Albee Foundation. He lives in California.

Paul Beckman

stories are widely published in print and online in the following magazines amongst others: *Connecticut Review*, *Raleigh Review*, *Litro*, *Playboy*, *PANK*, *Blue Fifth Review*, *Flash Frontier*, *Metazen*, *Boston Literary Magazine*, *Thrice Fiction* and *Literary Orphans*. His work has been in a number of anthologies and a dozen countries. His latest collection, *Peek*, published by Big Table Publishing weighed in at 65 stories and 120 pages. Find his website at www.paulbeckmanstories.com.

April Bradley

is from Goodlettsville, Tennessee and lives outside New Haven, Connecticut. Her work has appeared in *Boston Literary Magazine*, *Hermeneutic Chaos Literary Journal*, *Flash Frontier*, *Narratively*, and *Thrice Fiction*, among others. Her fiction recently has been nominated for the Best of the Net Anthology and for the Pushcart Prize. She is the Associate Editor for *Bartleby Snopes Literary Magazine and Press*. Find her online at aprilbradley.net.

Irene Buckler

has always enjoyed writing and making things. However, as a teacher, she concentrated on creating and writing educational programs and poetry. Now that she is retired, she is exploring other kinds of writing and flash fiction is her favourite. She loves the discipline involved in creating a complete story in so few words. Find Irene's sites at http://members.ozemail.com.au/~irenelesley/public_html/ and http://mudworks.weebly.com.

Guilie Castillo Oriard

is a Mexican writer and dog rescuer living in Curaçao. She misses Mexican food and Mexican *amabilidad*, but the laissez-faire attitude (and the beaches) are fair exchange. And the island's diversity provides great fodder for her obsession with culture clashes. Her work has appeared online and, in print, as part of *Pure Slush*'s *gorge* and *2014 A Year In Stories*. Her first book, *The Miracle of Small Things*, was published in August 2015 by Truth Serum Press. She's currently working on a full-length novel as well as several shorter projects. She blogs about life and writing at http://guilie-castillo-oriard.blogspot.com, and about life and dogs, at http://lifeindogs.blogspot.com.

Jessica Clements

studied English at the University of Adelaide. Her words have appeared in various Australian literary journals and online.

Mark Danowsky

has had his poetry appear in *Alba, Cordite, The Lake, Mobius, Red River Review, Shot Glass Journal* and else-where. Mark is originally from the Philadelphia area, but currently resides in North-Central West Virginia. He works for a private detective agency and is Managing Editor for the *Schuylkill Valley Journal*.

Gay Degani

has had three of her flash pieces nominated for Pushcart consideration and won the 11th Glass Woman Prize. Pure Slush Books released her collection of stories, *Rattle of Want*, in November 2015. Her suspense novel, *What Came Before*, was published in 2014 and a short collection, *Pomegranate*, features eight stories around the theme of mothers and daughters. Founder and editor emeritus of *Flash Fiction Chronicles*, she blogs at *Words in Place* where a complete list of her published work can be found.

Doug D'Elia

was born in Holyoke, Massachusetts. He is a graduate of the University of Central Florida, and served as a medic during the Vietnam War. He is the author of three books of poetry, one of short stories, and his plays have been performed in five states. He can be found on Facebook at Doug Delia, and his web page is dougdelia.com.

Mira Desai

lives, works and writes in Mumbai. She's published a translated novel and a volume of translated poems, in addition to fiction and non-fiction published online, in print and in several anthologies. She's recently stepped back from a lifetime in pharmaceuticals to pursue other interests.

Matt DeVirgiliis

enjoys life with his wife and two daughters in Point Pleasant, New Jersey. He has written and produced television shows for The Discovery Channel, TLC and Baby First Television. His short stories can be read on *Fictionaut*, *Istanbul Literary Review*, 52/250 *A Year of Flash* and on his site at mattdevirgiliis.wordpress.com.

Peter DiChellis

writes short mystery and suspense fiction. His sinister and sometimes comedic tales appear in several anthologies and ezines. He is a member of the Short Mystery Fiction Society and an Active (published author) member of the Private Eye Writers of America. For more, visit his site *Murder and Fries* at http://murderandfries.wordpress.com/.

William Doreski

lives in Peterborough, New Hampshire, and teaches at Keene State College. His most recent book of poetry is *The Suburbs of Atlantis* (2013). He has published three critical studies, including *Robert Lowell's Shifting Colors*. His essays, poetry, fiction, and reviews have appeared in many journals.

R. Gerry Fabian

is a retired English instructor. He has been publishing poetry since 1972 in various poetry magazines. His webpage is https://rgerryfabian.wordpress.com. His novel *Memphis Masquerade* is available at Smashwords and all other eBook stores, and he is editor of *Raw Dog Press:* http://www.rawdogpress.freesite2you.com/index.php.

Allen Forrest (illustrator)

has created cover art and illustrations for literary publications and books, has won the Leslie Jacoby Honor for Art at San Jose State University's *Reed Magazine*, and his Bel Red painting series is part of the Bellevue College Foundation's permanent art collection. Forrest's expressive drawing and painting style is a mix of avant-garde expressionism and post-Impressionist elements, creating emotion on canvas. You can find more of his work here: http://www.art-grafiken.blogspot.ca/.

Brad Garber

has degrees in biology, chemistry and law. He writes, paints, draws, photographs, hunts for mushrooms and snakes, and runs around naked in the Great Northwest. Since 1991, he has published poetry, essays and weird stuff in such publications as *Edge Literary Journal, Clementine Poetry Journal, Sugar Mule, Barrow Street, Aji Magazine* and other quality publications. He is a 2013 Pushcart Prize nominee.

Walter Giersbach

bounces between genres, from mystery to humor, speculative fiction to romance with some historical non-fiction thrown in for good measure. His work has appeared in print and online in over two dozen publications. Two volumes of short stories, *Cruising the Green of Second Avenue*, are available at Barnes & Noble, Amazon and other online booksellers. He's also bounced from Fortune 500 firms to university posts, and from homes in eight states and a couple of Asian countries.

Richard Mark Glover

has published short stories with *Oyster Boy Review, Crack the Spine, The Bookends Review, Sinister Tales, Canary,* and won the 2004 Eugene Walters Short Story Award. His journalism has appeared in the *San Antonio Express-News, West Hawaii Today, Ke Ola* and the *Big Bend Sentinel* where he won the 2010 Texas Press Association Best Feature Award, medium size weekly.

Lori Gravley

has lived in seven US states, visited nine African countries, lived in 39 houses, and traveled through 42 states. She's flown over 82,523 miles this year and driven 16,535 miles. She lives in a 125-year-old house in Yellow Springs, Ohio with one husband and two dogs. Her two grown children sometimes visit. She updates www.lorigravley.com five times a year and has posted almost 1,000 pictures @lorigravley on Instagram.

Jason Half-Pillow

has had his writing appear in *Abstract Jam, Dirty Chai, Crack The Spine, Driftwood Press, Dappled Things* and elsewhere. He has stories coming out soon in other publications as well, including *Cowboy Jamboree, Icarus Down Review,* and *The Intentional.*

Daniel Y. Harris

is the author of *The Underworld of Lesser Degrees* (NYQ Books, 2015) *Esophagus Writ* (with Rupert M. Loydell, The Knives Forks and Spoons Press, 2014), *Hyperlinks of Anxiety* (Cervena Barva Press, 2013), *The New Arcana* (with John Amen, NYQ Books, 2012), *Paul Celan and the Messiah's Broken Levered Tongue* (with Adam Shechter, Cervena Barva Press, 2010) and *Unio Mystica* (Cross-Cultural Communications, 2009).

Mark Hudson

is a poet and short story writer who has been published on the internet and in anthologies. To get a good idea of his poetry, go to *Illinoispoes.org.* He is also a frequent contributor to *Rockford Review* and *Greywolfe* anthologies in Michigan. He is delighted to be published by an Australian litmag, and hopes you enjoy his humorous "five" poem as well.

A.J. Huffman

has had poetry, fiction, haiku, and photography appear in hundreds of national and international journals, including *Labletter, The James Dickey Review,* and *Offerta Speciale,* in which her work appeared in both English and Italian translation. She is also the founding editor of Kind of a Hurricane Press: www.kindofahurricanepress.com

Phillis Ideal

both writes and paints, finding one no easier than the other. Her short stories are based on personal encounters in New York City and memories of growing up in New Mexico. She is a retired painting professor and has taught painting at UC Berkeley, San Francisco State and Sarah Lawrence. She is currently exhibiting in galleries and museums in the USA and in Europe and splits her time between NYC and Santa Fe. She was born in Roswell, New Mexico. Her stories have been published on *Pure Slush* (print and online) *Fictionaut, Santa Fe Literary Review*, and *Eunola Review*. You can contact her at pideal@earthlink.net.

Abha Iyengar

is an internationally published author, poet, editor and British Council certified creative writing facilitator. Her story, *The High Stool*, was nominated for the Story South Million Writers Award. She won the Lavanya Sankaran fellowship in 2009-10. She was a finalist in the *FlashMob* 2013 Flash Fiction contest. Her published works are *Yearnings*, Shrayan, *Flash Bites*, *Many Fish to Fry*, and *The Gourd Seller and Other Stories*. Find her blog here: http://abhaencounter.blogspot.in

Joanne Jagoda

retired in 2009, and one inspiring writing workshop launched her on her writing journey. Joanne's short stories, poetry and nonfiction appear in e-zines and print anthologies including *Pure Slush, Poetica, Persimmon Tree Magazine*. In 2015 she was nominated for a Pushcart Prize. Joanne enjoys Zumba, traveling and hanging with her five grandchildren, three of whom live in Jerusalem. Her blog,

My Detour, chronicles her nine month treatment for breast cancer which she has happily completed.

Christine Johnson

is an emerging writer. Writing follows sixteen years as a professional theatre director, in mainstream, community and young people's theatre. Completing a manuscript of her first full-length novel, she received an *Amplify your Art* grant (administered by Accessible Arts, NSW Government) in 2014 to work with a professional editor, developing skills to strengthen the work. Her prize-winning shorter fiction has been published around Australia and in the USA.

Len Kuntz

is a writer from Washington State and an editor at the online magazine *Literary Orphans*. His story collection *The Dark Sunshine* debuted from Connotation Press in 2014. You can also find him at lenkuntz.blogspot.com.

Hillary Leftwich

lives in Denver with her son where she is the associate editor for the *Conium Review*. In her day jobs she has worked as a private investigator, maid and pinup model. Her stories can be found in *NANO Fiction*, *Monkeybicycle*, *Dogzplot*, *Euonia Review*, *Progenitor*, *The Citron Review*, *WhiskeyPaper* and *Hobart*. She would like to thank her writing tribe Fishtankwriters for their support. You can find her on Twitter @HillaryLeftwich.

Denny E. Marshall

has had art, poetry, and fiction published. One recent credit is poetry in *Scifaikuest* November 2015. See more of Denny's work at www.dennymarshall.com.

Jolene McIlwain

teaches literary theory and analysis part-time at Chatham and Duquesne Universities in Pittsburgh, Pennsylvania. She writes and lives with her husband and son in the hills of the Appalachian Plateau, where myth and legends run deep as the coal seams and steady as the springs. Her work has been selected as Top 25 finalist for *Glimmer Train*'s Very Short Fiction prize.

Todd McKie

is an artist and writer. He lurches from canvas to keyboard, bleary-eyed and paint-spattered, but grateful for the exercise. His stories have appeared in *PANK*, *McSweeney's Internet Tendency*, *STORY* (Online), *Chicago Literati*, and elsewhere. Todd lives in Boston and blogs sporadically at toddmckie.blogspot.com.

Heather McQuillan

is a writer and writing tutor from Christchurch, New Zealand. Her flash fiction regularly appears in *Flash Frontier*. She also writes poetry, and novels for children. She is currently engaged in retelling the stories of migrant children who have arrived in Christchurch since the recent earthquakes. You can find more on Heather's profile at http://authors.org.nz/author/heathermcquillan/

Corey Mesler

has published in numerous anthologies and journals including *Poetry*, *Gargoyle*, *Five Points*, *Good Poems American Places*, and *Esquire/Narrative*. He has published 8 novels, 4 short story collections, and 5 full-length poetry collections. His latest novel, *Memphis Movie*, is from Soft Skull Press. He's been nominated for the Pushcart many times, and 2 of his poems were chosen for Garrison Keillor's

Writer's Almanac. With his wife he runs a bookstore in Memphis. His website: https://coreymesler.wordpress.com.

Neila Mezynski

resides in San Jose, California, a one time ballet dancer and choreographer turned abstract painter and author. Her fiction and poetry has appeared in many places including *Bewildering Stories*, *Snow Monkey Journal*, *Word Riot*, *Mud Luscious*, *Foundling Review*, *Weird Year*, and *Breadcrumb Sins*, among others.

Gwendolyn Joyce Mintz

is a writer and photographer, whose work has appeared in various journals and anthologies. She sews teddy bears by hand and reads when she can. She blogs (infrequently) at http://wwwonewriter.blogspot.com.

Sharon Lask Munson

grew up in Detroit, Michigan. After college she taught school in England, Germany, Okinawa, and Puerto Rico before driving to Anchorage, Alaska where she put down roots and taught for the next twenty years. She is the author of the chapbook, *Stillness Settles Down the Lane* (Uttered Chaos Press, 2010), a full-length book of poems, *That Certain Blue* (Blue Light Press, 2011), and *Braiding Lives* (Poetica Publishing, 2014). She lives and writes in Eugene, Oregon. Find her website at www.sharonlaskmunson.com.

Mandy Nicol

grew up in Melbourne and now lives in rural Victoria, Australia, with many four-legged friends and a duck named Doris. She works part time to support said four- and waddle-legged friends, and finds writing helps her to avoid doing the housework. Mandy has had stories published by *Pure Slush* in print and online.

Richard King Perkins II

is a state-sponsored advocate for residents in long-term care facilities. He lives in Crystal Lake, IL, USA with his wife, Vickie and daughter, Sage. He is a three-time Pushcart nominee and a Best of the Net nominee whose work has appeared in more than a thousand publications.

Matt Potter

is an Australian-born writer who keeps a part of his psyche in Berlin. Matt has been published in various places online, and he is, rather amazingly, also the founding editor of *Pure Slush*. You can find more of his work including details of his travel memoir *Hamburgers and Berliners and other courses in between* (Cervena Barva Press, 2015) at his website http://mattcpotter.webs.com/.

Darryl Price

has published dozens of chapbooks, and his poems have appeared in many journals.

Stephen V. Ramey

lives in beautiful New Castle, Pennsylvania, with his wife and two reformed feral cats. His work has appeared in many places, including *The Journal of Compressed Creative Arts*, *The Doctor T. J. Eckleburg Review*, and *Every Day Fiction*. His collection of (very) short fictions, *Glass Animals* (Pure Slush Books), is available wherever fine books are e-sold. Find more at www.stephenvramey.com and on Facebook and twitter (@svramey).

Shannon Coghlan Reiss

is an American writer and communications specialist from Philadelphia. She received her BA in English and Masters in Leadership Development while working in marketing, communications, and medical publishing. She has been writing fiction for over twenty-five years and is now editing a collection of short stories while studying literature in Paris, France. Find Shannon online at www.shannoncoghlan.com.

Sally Reno

lives in a vaporish grotto where she serves as Pythoness to *Blink Ink Print* and Haruspex for *Shining Mountains Press*. Her fiction has been among the winners of National Public Radio's 3-Minute Fiction Contest, the *Moon Milk Review* Prosetry Contest, and has been nominated for the Pushcart Prize.

Helia Rethmann

grew up in Germany, but now lives in Nashville, TN, where she teaches, writes and cleans up after too many animals. Her fiction has most recently appeared in *Intrinsick Magazine* and in *Virgins*, a Penn Family Publication.

Alex Robertson

was born in Adelaide and has spent his working life around (country) South Australia and the Northern Territory. He has been writing poetry since his teenage years, occasionally published first in university student publications and then in journals. Since his relocation to outer Adelaide, he has tried his hand at short stories for his own interest. He is also involved in writing groups in Gawler and the North East suburbs of Adelaide.

Ruth Sabath Rosenthal

is a New York poet, well-published in literary journals and poetry anthologies throughout the U.S. and internationally. In October 2006, her poem *on yet another birthday* was nominated for a Pushcart prize by *Ibbetson Street Magazine*. Ruth has authored five books of poetry: *Facing Home* (a chapbook); *Facing Home and beyond; little, but by no means small; Food: Nature vs Nurture;* and *Gone, but Not Easily Forgotten.* Purchase these books from amazon.com, or ruthspoems@aol.com. For more about Ruth, visit her website at www.newyorkcitypoet.com.

Barbara Ruth

writes at the convergence of Ashkenazi Jewish and Potowatomee, fat and yogi, disabled and neuroqueer, not this and not that. Her photography, memoirs, poems and fiction appear in the following anthologies published in 2015 and 2016: *Barking Sycamores: Best of the First Year; Yellow Chair Anthology; QDA: Queer Disability Anthology: Lunessence; Garland of the Goddess; Slim Volume: This Body I Live Inside; Spoon/Knife Reader.*

Martin Shaw

quotes Elton John: "Born and raised a proper, I guess life just bugged him."

Allison Sobczak

is a graduate of Columbia College Chicago where she earned a BA in Creative Writing. Her work has appeared in *Columbia College Literary Review, Hot Metal Bridge, Rollick Magazine, Intrinsick Magazine, 1:1000* and *805 Lit + Art.* She grew up in a small suburban town in Pennsylvania, but the Windy City has become her second home. Follow her blog at allisonsobczak.com.

Andrew Stancek

grew up in Bratislava and saw tanks rolling through its streets. He currently dreams and entertains Muses in southwestern Ontario. His work has appeared in *Tin House* online, *Journal of Compressed Creative Arts, Vestal Press, Every Day Fiction, fwriction,* and *Camroc Press Review,* among others. He's been a winner in the Flash Fiction Chronicles and Gemini Fiction Magazine contests and been nominated for a Pushcart Prize.

Nancy Stohlman

is the creator and curator of the Fbomb Flash Fiction Reading Series in Denver, and her work has been nominated for a 2016 Pushcart Prize. Her books include *The Vixen Scream and other Bible Stories*, *The Monster Opera*, *Searching for Suzi: a flash novel*, and four anthologies including *Fast Forward: The Mix Tape*, a finalist for a 2011 Colorado Book Award. Find more at her website here: www.nancystohlman.com.

Jan Elman Stout

is a native Chicagoan who lives with her family in Washington, D.C. She is a flash fiction and short story writer and has been published in *Literary Orphans*.

Tim Suermondt

is the author of two full-length collections of poems: *Trying to Help the Elephant Man Dance* (The Backwaters Press, 2007) and *Just Beautiful* (New York Quarterly Books, 2010.) His third collection *Election Night and the Five Satins* will be published early in 2016 by Glass Lyre Press. He has poems published in *Poetry*, *The Georgia Review*, *Prairie Schooner*, *Ploughshares*, *Blackbird*, *Bellevue Literary Review*, *PANK*, *North Dakota Quarterly*, *december magazine*, *Plume Poetry Journal* and *Stand Magazine* (U.K.) among others. He lives in Cambridge (MA) with his wife, the poet Pui Ying Wong.

Susan Tally

has had poems published in *Clementine*, *Melancholy Hyperbole* and *Birds Piled Loosely*. She lives in New York City where she enjoys tutoring young children in a literacy program.

Susan Tepper

is the author of six published books of fiction and poetry. Most current is her novel-in-stories *The Merrill Diaries* (Pure Slush Books, 2013). Her newest book is a linked-flash collection *dear Petrov* to be released by Pure Slush Books in February of 2016. Tepper has been a writer for twenty years. She writes a column called Let's Talk at *Black Heart Magazine*, where she also does author/book interviews. FIZZ, her reading series, has been ongoing for eight years at KGB Bar, NYC. Find her website at www.susantepper.com.

Townsend Walker

draws inspiration from cemeteries, foreign places, violence and strong women. A novella in noir, *La Ronde,* was published by Truth Serum Press in June 2015. Some seventy short stories have been published in literary journals. Awards: first place in the SLO NightWriters contest, second place in *Our Stories* contest, two nominations for the PEN / O. Henry Award. Four stories were performed at the New Short Fiction Series in Hollywood.

Michael Webb

blogs at http://michaelwebb.us and can be found chasing rainbows and rooting for the Boston Red Sox in suburban Philadelphia, Pennsylvania.

Anne E. Weisgerber

wishes Eric Fischl hadn't removed his Tumbling Woman (2002) sculpture from display. She has recent stories published or forthcoming in *The Airgonaut, Tahoma Literary Review, The Journal of Compressed Creative Arts, Vignette Review,* and *Jellyfish Review.* She is a freelance fiction editor. When not teaching, she's working on a novel that spans five generations. Follow her @AEWeisgerber, or visit anneweisgerber.com.

Diana J.Wynne

tells it like it is. Her stories about politics, identity, travel, and the Kennedy assassination have appeared in *The New York Times*, *Salon*, *Litro*, *Raw Story*, *storySouth*, *Mississippi Review*, *Chicago Literati*, and of course *Pure Slush*. She lives in San Francisco and blogs at The Daily Interface (chestnutdrive.com) and One is a wanderer (bigbadbeautifulworld.blogspot.com). Make her an offer.

Other books from Pure Slush

Visit the Pure Slush Store:
http://pureslush.webs.com/store.htm

Feast!
ISBN: 978-1-925101-62-1

dear Petrov
ISBN: 978-1-925101-69-0

Rattle of Want
ISBN: 978-1-925101-67-6

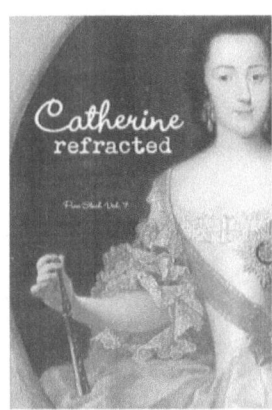  

Catherine refracted
ISBN: 978-1-925101-78-2

The Vixen Scream
ISBN: 978-1-925101-11-9

Many Fish to Fry
ISBN: 978-1-925101-59-1